SPANISH PORTRAIT

by

ELIZABETH LAKE

LONDON
PILOT PRESS LTD
1945

First published by
PILOT PRESS LTD., 45, *Great Russell Street, London, W.C.*1,
December, 1945.

Second Impression March, 1946.

*This book is produced in complete
conformity with the authorised economy
standards.*

PRINTED BY
METCALFE & COOPER, LTD.,
WOOL EXCHANGE, LONDON, E.C.2.

CONTENTS

PART ONE

SAN SEBASTIAN. AUTUMN 1934

1

ONE bright morning a shiny Chrysler drew up outside a block of flats which looked like white cardboard in the hard sunlight. The Chrysler was driven by a young Spaniard. He was in the Diplomatic Service and he might have been an advertisement, with his wavy dark hair, handsome sunburnt face and well-cut, well-pressed grey flannel suit.

Shutting one eye and shading the other with a brown hand, he pressed down the hooter and looked fixedly up at the balcony of the sixth floor. Minutes passed while he sounded the hooter again and again. Then frowning and whistling a paso-doble he got out, slammed the door and dashed into the lift. Outside the door of the sixth floor flat he hesitated and then rang the bell.

The grille clicked open, a pair of eyes surveyed him, the grille shut and slowly the door opened. A young girl came out on to the stone landing.

" Why it's Manolo ! " she said with exaggerated surprise. " It's all right. They're all out."

" I suppose that's why you didn't look over the balcony when I sounded the hooter," said Manolo. " You thought you'd make me come up."

" Oh no ! I didn't think you were coming."

" You must have heard me."

" So many cars go by—how was I to know ? "

" I thought we'd arranged it."

" The last thing I expected was that you'd be punctual."

He propped himself against the wall.

" I suppose you've still got your hangover," she said, acidly. " Or is it another one ? "

" I went to bed early and didn't drink anything."

Maria (for that was her name, although she was English) said nothing, still fuming at his behaviour of the previous day, the feast of San Fermin. Their plan had been to see the celebrations at Pamplona where bulls were let loose in the streets in the morning and amateurs could try their luck with a few passes, where there were Carnival processions and a series of bullfights in the afternoon given by the best toreros. A start should have been made at seven. Maria was ready in good time, but Manolo did not arrive till ten, nodding with sleep and fretful with a painful hangover. Her cousin Ethel had gone, too, to chaperone them, and had mumbled about unpunctuality all the way. The ride to Pamplona was alarming, the road wound around hills with deep declines on one side. Manolo fell half asleep at the wheel and once they nearly went over into a deep ravine. His reply to her fear was " Almost as exciting as seeing the bulls ! " At Roncesvalles there was a halt in order to look down through the wooded, precipitous slopes on to the dramatic setting of Roland's last hours, while Manolo recited a long piece about the episode. Maria had put an end to this with " What about getting to Pamplona ? " which annoyed Manolo. No more was said until they reached the outskirts of the town, when they had lunch in the orchard of an inn.

The lunch was delicious, the sun was hot and immediately he had finished, Manolo had said, " Now for a siesta under the trees," looking at both Maria and Ethel as though he didn't give a damn what they thought.

Maria decided to herself, " That clinches it. I shall never take him seriously again, in spite of the Chrysler and everything else," but said nothing and left the nagging to Ethel, who insisted that they should go on to Pamplona and see what was left of the feast.

There was little to see when they arrived, no bulls ran through the streets, Manolo's arrangements about tickets for the fight had gone astray because he was too late and they had been passed on to someone else, and though a few, great, nodding Carnival figures paraded the streets the cafés were so over-crowded that no seats could be had from which to see the procession. Finally, Ethel was left in a dingy café in a side street where nothing was going on, while Maria and Manolo hired two horrible bathing costumes and went for a swim in the river.

Maria commented, " We could have had a better swim in the sea where we came from."

She was bitterly disappointed. For weeks he had described eloquently the great events of this day. She had fought hard to be allowed to spend the whole day with a Spaniard, and had been given permission only on condition that Ethel went, too, and now Ethel would be thinking that the whole thing was a put up job, that Manolo had only used the feast as an excuse for getting Maria to himself for a whole day, and that they wouldn't have gone to Pamplona at all if Ethel hadn't gone too. All this was certain to be said or hinted at later. It was a big price to pay for nothing but a miserable swim.

On the way home Manolo was penitent. He apologised and asked Maria if she could ever forgive him. His hangover had gone and his head was clear.

" What would be the use of *forgiving* you ? " she said, " I've missed the feast of San Fermin. I may never have the chance of seeing it again."

" Oh yes you will, with me, in three years' time."

She shook her head.

And now, as she stood on the landing watching him, her indignation made her silent.

He suggested a quick spin in the car, and when she refused this invitation, urged her to meet him in the evening for a drink. Whenever he felt sure of her he was unpunctual and unreliable, she thought, and when she was difficult he became most attentive. She declined the offer of a drink, but then realising that the break with him would come anyhow, as he was off to Shanghai in a few days, and she could never write letters, and that once he was gone she would know no one in San Sebastian except the people in the flat, and life with them was not amusing, she thought better of it.

" I suppose you couldn't bring this friend of yours, Alonso, along, too," she said, " I'd like to meet him before you go. I think perhaps I could meet you after my last lesson."

" That's splendid," he said, " I'll try and bring him along."

Manolo was a generous hearted character, full of enthusiasm about his friends. He had spoken so glowingly of Alonso to her, had quoted so many of his remarks that at last she was intrigued. He had been described as a " huge, rather ugly man," " a flashing wit," " a great painter," " an independent mind." At the same time she remembered how many things which Manolo had talked of so often and so eloquently had turned to dust and ashes and she wondered.

He took his leave of her, kissed her hand and dashed down the stairs.

2

The meeting took place in Sacha, a select café which looked on to the Bulevar. From five o'clock onwards smartly dressed young women with their mothers or other suitable chaperones would sit here drinking weak tea with lemon and surreptitiously watch the groups of young and middle aged men in expensive suits who sat at the bar drinking American cocktails. The modern decorations, the chromium plate and the rows of tiny, exquisite cakes in the window gave Sacha an air of affluence and gaiety to which its clientèle responded.

Manolo was determined that his two stars should not fail to see each other's brightness and was working very hard, drawing them out, laughing at everything they said, and urging them to try special cocktails.

" Doesn't she speak Castillian like a native ? " he said.

" Yes, very well indeed," said Alonso, remote as a sleepy cat behind the smoke of his cigar, and he smiled as though he was thinking of something else or nothing at all.

Manolo had started a political talk which he had meant to be light, but Maria was bent on arguing with him.

"The sort of democracy you mean," she said, "is neither here nor there. I'm sick of hearing how fundamentally democratic Spain is, whereas the English are snobs. I wouldn't have expected you, who call yourself an Anarchist, to take that line. It's the standard of living that counts. Just because some of your dukes and marquises make jokes with their chauffeurs or play chess with fishermen in cafés you say they're democratic. They underpay the chauffeurs they joke with, if the fishermen strike for more pay, they mow them down—and they'd never dream of bringing them home to their families. And even this phoney democracy only exists among the men. Upper class women don't attempt to be nice to anyone except people more classy than themselves."

Manolo looked attentive. Alonso watched the people in the Bulevar. As she spoke, she found herself contrasting Manolo's *jeune premier* good looks with Alonso's flat, shiny, placid, oval face.

"Perhaps you're right," said Manolo. "They're medieval, they—the men, I mean—treat the lower classes well as long as they know their place, the idea of a hierarchy is very ingrained. But when it comes to a strike, they're furious, they're outraged."

Alonso leant across the table and said with a smile, "I like strikes. It's so nice when there aren't any buses or trams !"

"Why ?" asked Maria.

"One doesn't feel guilty about taking taxis."

"All strikes aren't bus and tram strikes," said Maria.

"Well, those are the ones I like best, then." Alonso sank back into his chair.

"Haven't you any sympathy at all with the strikers, apart from feeling less guilty about taxis ?" she went on.

Manolo intervened. "He pretends he's terribly reactionary," he laughed, "but we'll find him on the right side of the barricades when the time comes."

"What makes you think that ?" said Alonso.

Manolo changed the subject. "Maria appreciates our wonderful country. Basque country, green and fertile, undulating, friendly and yet mysterious. I have told her all about the Druid's rites . . . and the witches' Sabbaths which still go on here."

He certainly had. On their excursions through the Basque country every bit of mistletoe had been connected with secret rites. Whole afternoons had been spent going through the villages on the border of Guipuzcoa and Navarre looking for traces of a witches' Sabbath. He was an ardent Basque Nationalist besides being an Anarchist. "All Basques are natural Anarchists," he often declared. He also believed that all Basques were aristocrats because the humblest family in the humblest village had its coat of arms, and therefore he would conclude there was really no class distinction, and it was only the titled families from the South who came for the season to the Basque coast who behaved so arrogantly and created a bad impression. He upheld the idea of a strong, provincial nationalism and insisted that it was different from the other sort of nationalism which was going on in Germany.

Alonso looked exasperated. "Druids! Druids! Why should anyone like the Basque country because it once had Druids?"

Manolo took this as a joke. "I don't take Druids as seriously as you think!"

"I never said you took them seriously—but you mention them so often."

"We never saw any sign of them," said Maria, "no sign of any kind of witchcraft. I don't believe there is any or ever was any." She suddenly felt ashamed of siding against Manolo, when they ought to be allied against Alonso's high-handed, indolent manner. "If there ever was any, I mean, there aren't any traces of it now."

3

Maria had plenty of time to think over this meeting as she walked back along the whole length of the Concha to her flat. She felt furious with Alonso and decided he was a typical specimen of the Spanish upper class, conceited, arrogant, unaware that their day was done, even though the fall of the monarchy should have warned them.

The beach was almost deserted at this time of day, although the water would be at its best. In the morning it was so crowded that no one could sunbathe properly, and children kept getting lost in the crowd. Descriptions of them would be broadcast by the announcer who was stationed in a light pavilion-like structure known as " the Pearl of the Ocean," overhanging the centre of the beach and containing a dance floor, a restaurant and a wireless station. The Concha beach was used by the middle classes in the morning and by the less prosperous in the afternoon.

Above the beach was a pretty promenade and a number of girls, many of them dazzling beauties with flashing black eyes and hair like thick lacquer, were walking up and down in small groups, enjoying the soft, warm evening air and preparing for the successes of the evening parade. " The upper class girls try to look as though they're there by chance," thought Maria, " on their way to Benediction or some late shopping." The others laughed and talked in rich, harsh voices and looked quite openly to see what effect they were making on the young men who lolled against the railings.

Maria, an orphan brought up by a widowed aunt, had first come to San Sebastian in the Spring of 1933 in order to learn Spanish to get a scholarship. Her aunt could not afford to give her more than the money for her fare and so she supported herself by being governess to the children of a well-known San Sebastian lawyer. Manolo was a distant connection of theirs and had met her there. The unruliness of the children and the unpredictable temperament of their mother who flew into a rage if any gentleman of her acquaintance appeared to take any interest in Maria, had been too much for her and this year she had

resolved to give lessons and be independent. But her present
independence was very small because her cousin Ethel had been
sent with her to chaperone her and they were both living with
an elderly English woman, called Miss Pearson, one time
governess to the children of a Grandee.

Her flat was in Ondarreta, the most fashionable part of the
town. Ondarreta had a small beach of its own, more select than
the Concha and less crowded. The families who frequented the
beach mostly knew each other and maintained a very high
standard of decency in bathing costumes. Women wore skirts
down to the knees and short sleeves and men did not expose
their chests. The blue blooded seldom broke this rule, but a few
emancipated sons and daughters of the rich professional classes
did, in moderation. Two old men in khaki, looking like ex-
soldiers, hovered around the tents looking for indecent dress,
and Maria had once seen them go up to a woman and make her
leave the beach because she was wearing a two-piece suit. All
through the summer priests would thunder from the pulpit
against the indecency of the beach, urging Ondarreta to set a
good example to the Concha where one would soon see the same
licence as in Biarritz and Saint Jean de Luz. When Maria
pointed out to Miss Pearson that in England the most respectable people bathed without skirts, the answer was, " The Spanish
are very hot blooded." Grimly overhanging one end of the beach
was a prison, a plain, dark stone building with small barred
windows.

At the other end, raised between Ondarreta and the Concha,
was the royal palace built by Alfonso XIII, and empty since his
abdication, an ugly building, well set in a large park and com-
manding a magnificent view of the curved bay and the island of
Santa Clara.

The high spot in the social life of Ondarreta was the tennis
club, meeting place of the " señoritos," and of wealthy tourists
and people with money who were socially on the make. Here an
atmosphere of freedom and up-to-dateness was created by an
interest in sport, the wearing of sports clothes and the speaking
of English and French. Real old diehards still disapproved of
this place, and did not often allow their daughters to go there,

ven with a chaperone. Manolo, too, disliked it, and told Maria
many stories of the " señoritos " (mainly the young men of
southern families, he insisted, not Basques) who never did a
stroke of work the whole year round, paid court to wealthy
girls and seduced pretty shop assistants whom they would leave
high and dry, called themselves monarchists, were abysmally
ignorant but liked to use English words because that showed a
love of sport and also that one's family had been exalted enough
to have an English governess.

Maria gave two lessons every day and sometimes three. The
first was with two girls who were going to study at Madrid
University. Their family was not well off and they were very
hard working. The eldest one had a prodigious memory and
could learn long vocabularies by heart in ten minutes. They
were very thoughtful and always gave her the most comfortable
chair. Her second pupil was the small round son of a duchess.
He would sit in Miss Pearson's drawing room, his legs dangling,
half asleep after a huge lunch. He was a lazy, good natured little
boy. There was an understanding between them that it was
only a whim of his mother's that he should learn English ;
providing the marks went up a little each week, everyone would
be satisfied and no one need do much work. She would make
him read English for ten minutes, accepting his peculiar, nasal
pronunciation so completely that she never thought of correcting
him, and spoke to him with his own accent to make it easier.

The third lesson was the most trying. This was to a girl of
fifteen who had been to school in London and Paris, and was a
member of the tennis club and girls' hockey team, and she
would speak of sports unendingly, thinking that Maria must
like this because all English people did. She was very well
groomed and extremely rich, with a sitting room of her own on
the second floor of her father's huge villa. On a small table was
a portrait of Alfonso XIII, two lighted candles and a bowl of
flowers. She had seen Maria out with Manolo, and her rather
tactless remarks showed that she thought him far too well
connected to be running round with an English teacher. Her
manner fluctuated between offensiveness and showing off in an
ingratiating way. The way she spoke to the servants made

Maria's blood boil. Her favourite English book was " The
Rosary."

Maria also exchanged lessons with Señor Jaime Torre, a thin
and wiry Andalusian tutor. He was a good teacher with a soft
Southern accent and was more interested in teaching her
Spanish than in learning English. He talked about himself most
of the time. " I have been in love once," he told her, " but in
love as only we Andalusians understand it. If any other man had
approached my sweetheart I should have killed him." He
described his courtship in a town near Seville and its background of jasmine, nard and guitars. He had parted with his
sweetheart because they were both too proud to make up a
quarrel. " I am a very proud man, as proud as a lion."

He said he was a great Don Juan, but no woman meant
anything to him now. He described his seductions at great
length, and took no notice when Maria tried to stop him (she
was terrified Miss Pearson would overhear one day). He was a
member of the right wing Gil Robles party and attended their
meetings, which were held in the basement of Maria's block of
flats. He was a fervent Catholic and oddly enough agreed with
the priests about the immorality of the beach. According to his
stories, he went about seducing every young girl he met, but he
said he would never dream of marrying anyone who was not a
virgin, because that was the greatest dishonour that could
befall any man.

He made a point of treating Maria in a very " caballero " way,
as he called it, and never let a lesson pass without saying something like, " I have the greatest respect for your knowledge of
Spanish literature," or " My feelings towards you are those of
the purest friendship," which was true.

4

Manolo was going to Shanghai for three years and he spent his last days in San Sebastian supervising his packing. He was taking most of his possessions, including a baby grand piano, a large gramophone and two huge cases of records. He adored practically all music, played the piano with enthusiasm and composed short pieces in the style of Debussy.

Miss Pearson was glad to hear he was going, because she thought he was a rake who lured Maria into drinking in cafés and going for excursions. " I know someone who knows a great deal about him." she would say and refuse to tell who it was, " He drinks and he chases after every girl he meets." She was so pleased to see the last of him that she allowed Maria to ask him to the flat on his last afternoon. He came while Miss Pearson and Ethel were having their siesta and was very excited about an idea he'd had.

" I am going to ask Alonso to paint you," he said, " and send the portrait off to me."

" I don't think he'll like that," said Maria.

" Oh yes he will. We are great friends, and he can hardly refuse."

" Well, he wasn't very friendly when I met him."

" Oh, that's just his odd manner. It doesn't mean anything. I've known him for years and understand him thoroughly. I'm determined he shall paint you. I would like a portrait and I want to feel you have someone intelligent to talk to when I go."

It certainly would liven up her life to get away from the flat occasionally and also she was still intrigued by Alonso. " Well, you can ask him. It's all the same to me whether he refuses or not."

Two days later a letter came from Manolo, sent off as he was about to embark. The proprietory ring of the opening " My little Maria " irritated her, but she was pleased to find as she read on, " Alonso will be delighted to paint you. He is a real friend and you will get to like him very much. He wants you to get in touch with him—he is in the phone book—and suggested Thursday at 11 for the first sitting. That will be in " Gu " (a

Basque word meaning us) a club for painters and sculptors. You will meet many distinguished Basque artists there."

When she phoned Alonso he didn't sound delighted, but he gave her vague directions how to get to " Gu " and said he would be there at eleven the next day.

5

Maria was punctual and found herself waiting outside the locked door of " Gu " for what seemed hours. Alonso arrived at last, bland and smiling, apologised for his lateness and explained, " I hardly ever get up before twelve."

He found a piece of cardboard on which he'd already begun a picture. " This will do," he said, placed her on a chair facing the light and began to scrutinise her face, first with one eye, then with the other and then with both. Nothing was said for a long time and then he came up to her, looked at her closely, offered her a cigarette and said, " You may smoke if you like."

" Thank you," said Maria, as sarcastically as she could, but he didn't notice it.

After more scrutiny and measuring, he made her change her position. Then followed a few polite remarks about the fine weather for Manolo's crossing.

When the sitting was over, he shook hands with her and hurried away, saying, " I think we'd better make it twelve tomorrow."

During the second sitting she felt depressed by the way he treated her. Although he looked at her the whole time, she might have been a still life for all the difference it made. Her fair hair and blue eyes had always produced an impression on Spaniards up till now. She thought it would be better to tell him he needn't go on with the portrait if he didn't want to, and she would tell Manolo there hadn't been enough time for it.

Alonso's face fascinated her.   At first he looked like a fat, massive Chinaman, but one soon noticed his features were perfectly modelled.   His skin was a pale, opaque yellow and his hair, taken straight back without a parting, was like a black cap. He was always composed.

There was a break of ten minutes while he smoked one of his small cigars.   " And what do you think of ' Gu ' ? " he said.

" It's very nice."

" How do you like the decorations ? "

She looked at a rose-madder winking sun on the lower panel of the door.   " I don't like that colour much, it's rather sickly and sentimental."

" Sentimental to the Nordic races but passionate to us," he smiled, and she knew he was laughing at her.

She arrived for the third sitting determined to make him change his attitude to her or to give up the portrait.

He was more talkative and made comments on " Gu," the weather, the awfulness of the beach and asked her how she liked San Sebastian.

" I don't like it at all except the port."

When it was time for a break, she said, looking down at the floor and trying to sound casual, " Let's go and have a drink."

" All right."   He laid down his brushes at once like a child who has been let off homework.   " That's a splendid idea. There's a café at the end of the street.   Do you want to see what I've done ? "

It was unfair to judge the picture at this early stage, but it looked to Maria like the beginning of a dull, accurate repro-duction of her features and colouring.   She was disappointed.

They stepped out into the Calle del Angel, which sloped below, broken by flights of steps to make the decline less sharp. It was narrow and there was no pavement.   The houses were old and half ruined and coloured clothes were hanging out to dry.

" If it were more Moorish it would be like Toledo," said Alonso.

" I've never been to Toledo.   I only know Guipuzcoa and Navarre."

They stopped at a large café which looked on to the back of

the casino. Gambling was no longer allowed since the fall of the Monarchy, but there was always a question of removing the ban because it was bad for the tourist trade. The gay building faced some flowerless gardens, prettily laid out with tiled benches and tamarind trees and overlooking the sea. The year before there had been gambling for two days, but the local authorities had stopped it despite the outcry in the papers.

A glass of pernod made Alonso more expansive. " And what do you think of the portrait ? " he asked.

" I think it's quite like me, but I don't like it as a picture, though of course you can't tell at this stage, and I know nothing about pictures."

" I'm not a good painter."

" But I've always heard you were."

" From Manolo, I suppose ? "

" He said it as though other people thought so, too."

He laughed, " Manolo always makes a legend out of his friends."

" But I daresay you are a good painter."

" I'm not. It's more and more obvious I'm not. I was an infant prodigy, and like the rest of my family taken in by my technical ability. When I was twelve I could do likenesses of anyone. I could paint as well as I do now—probably better— but I never had any ideas at all. So I stick to portraits, straightforward ordinary portraits—they don't need inspiration to reach a moderate standard."

" You're not very interested in painting me, are you ? "

" No, I'm not really."

" Is my face uninteresting ? "

He smiled at her kindly. " I don't want you to think I find it uninteresting, and it's certainly attractive in its way, but I think it would be best as a huge poster advertising tooth paste or soap." He shrugged his shoulders. " Still, there's nothing to be done about it now. It must be made as acceptable to Manolo's standards of beauty as possible. He's going to have it."

" What's the matter with my face from your point of view ? "

" It's too comprehensible. One knows the whole layout at first glance. Hollywood has simplified every type. A face now

has to stick in your mind like a jazz tune. Before, women had
more indeterminate faces."

"What about your own face?" said María, as the conversation seemed so candid, "I find it very perfect, but the
layout is obvious."

He looked delighted by the compliment. "As a painter, I'm
bound to admit my face is perfect, but I don't agree that it's
obvious. Men's faces can't be as obvious as women's because
they can't use make-up or pluck their eyebrows. Then, a very
blue jaw like mine lends an air of mystery."

She couldn't tell whether he was joking or not. "Do you
paint nothing but portraits?"

"Nothing but portraits, nearly always of elderly, rich ladies.
They pay well. I enjoy watching them. The eyebrows are
badly plucked and everything's out of shape. They have the
crazy inconsequent expression one sees in the moon's face or
in faces in the grain of wood or in the pattern on the wallpaper.
Great bulging surfaces between the eyebrow and the lid are
exposed, full of little holes where the hairs have been removed,
the constant use of cosmetics produces lovely big pores around
the nose and chin and there's a fine contrast between the lipstick
on the actual mouth and the lipstick above it where they try to
make their upper lips like rosebuds. That's how I'd like to
paint them, but I always do a nice, flattering picture. Now I
should like to paint you as a blur with all the emphasis on the
nose where there are delicate layers of skin peeling—the edges
are white, the surface brown, the underneath red."

"Why don't you do me like that? I shouldn't care?"

"And what would Manolo say?"

"I suppose you're a modern Valdes Leal," she said.

"Oh no. I don't paint decaying matter to point out the
platitude of the transitoriness of human beauty and I'm not
religious. I just like painting things I like."

"But you just said you didn't paint things you like."

"I know, but that's all I want to do. I haven't any ideas and
I haven't any problems. I'll never be much of a painter." He
was apparently cheerful about his limitations.

"It must be very nice to be you," she said. "You make me

feel as though I don't notice anything or enjoy it. When I see people with enlarged pores, my only reaction is to feel sorry for them. As for my own nose peeling, I've been miserable about that all through the summer. I only seem to like things there's some obvious reason for liking."

6

There was no more uneasiness. Maria and Alonso cut the next few sittings and met every day between her lessons. They took it for granted they would see each other whenever possible. They would sit in cafés or in " Gu " watching the painted boats lying in the harbour, and the great nets spread out to dry. Or they would walk round the port and see the tunny fish and sardines being unloaded. The fishwomen fought to be the first to fill their trays with sardines, and as soon as they were full would swing the trays on their heads and rush off down the streets shouting " Sardinas! "

Sometimes Alonso would act as guide and show her the old part of the town near the port, making up fantastic histories about the buildings which took his fancy.

Unlike other Spaniards, she had met, he never showed the least interest in England. He said that the idea of London enveloped in a pea soup fog with all the inhabitants divided into vivisectionists and anti-vivisectionists was good enough for him.

" But you've been to London," she protested.

" What makes you think that ? "

" Manolo told me."

He admitted he'd been to London when he was seventeen and lived in a boarding house near Finsbury Park. He was fascinated by the boarding house, the landlady and her family. The youngest daughter, a malnourished child of thirteen, always had a streaming cold, cotton wool in her ears and sometimes plaster on her cheeks. " Every time I met this little girl I wanted to give her an enormous hug." The elder daughter was so polite and had such delicate feelings that when her mother sent her up with the bill she blushed as she handed it to him and looked as though she might burst into tears. He said he had forgotten any English he had ever known.

Bit by bit she found out more about him. He was thirty, he had three sisters, he drank a great deal, nearly always pernod, he made quite a lot of money painting portraits, but he lost most of it in the Casino at Biarritz. Most of the time he seemed to have no ambition; but once, after several glasses of pernod, he said, " I should like to take a studio in Paris, get up early, paint all day with short breaks for meals, and then perhaps something would happen! " He added, " Of course, I never shall."

He came to San Sebastian only for the summer and lived in Madrid for the rest of the year at his father's house. His mother was dead, his father was wealthy and easy-going and often paid his debts for him.

He was fond of Manolo and assumed Maria was seriously tied up with him, but it amused him to provoke her into being dis- loyal. As they watched a tree-felling competition, he turned to her and said, laughing, " Manolo would have something to say about these fine Basque types, these rippling Basque muscles, wouldn't he ? "

" He'd say there is nothing more noble than manual labour."

Two fine, bronzed Basques were standing on a platform, each felling a log, swinging his axe steadily and rhythmically. They came from different villages of Guipuzcoa and were the semi- finalists. The spectators were excited and shouted at each stroke.

" It's Homeric," he said, " but I can't stand more than five minutes of it. I hope you write and tell him what typical things I'm showing you, tsistulari concerts, tree-felling competitions, the port, old monasteries."

He surprised her one day by saying he must get on with the portrait. " If I do a little every day, I'll soon get through it."

" Don't you mind painting it now ? "

" I like seeing you so much that it doesn't matter whether I'm painting or not."

No remark had ever pleased her so much. " Why do you like seeing me ? "

" Because you're very nice, although you ask me an enormous number of questions. I leave you feeling I've done an examination paper, and when I go home I feel I should swat for the next day's."

" I suppose you just feel flattered. You'd like anyone who asked you questions all the time. And I prided myself on having got you to talk at all."

" Ah, but nobody asks me questions like that. There aren't many people so thorough as you." He looked at her affectionately. " And when are you going to give me my marks ? When are you going to tell me whether I passed or failed ? What do you do with all these answers ? "

" I don't know."

" There you are, you see, when it comes to being asked a few questions yourself you don't come out so well. Remember that before you give me my results."

7

One Sunday evening, when there was no lesson to give, she walked with him to the park near the station. It was a sombre place surrounded by small, grimy factories and warehouses, and enclosed by tall, rusty railings. The park and the thought that she was leaving for England very soon now made Maria feel melancholy. They stood by the dirty lake and watched a swan float by.

" I don't really like swans," she said, " unless their necks are curved back and their wings half open, they're so badly balanced."

" You should have been a painter with ideas like that," he mocked her, " though women don't make good painters. Now there was one girl with a lot of talent, she used to live just over there, a very interesting girl."

" How was she interesting ? "

" Oh, she had a lot of life.   She was original."

" Oh! ". She felt jealous.

" She asked me to meet her in her garden one evening, and she came running out of the house and gave me some bitter leaves to eat and said they were delicious. When I'd eaten one, she laughed and ran off again. She was a surrealist with a complex about her father, and all her pictures were about that. There was always a huge man in them with her father's face, stuffing children into his mouth or sitting talking to horrible reptiles."

" Did she have any success ? "

" No. She was going to give an exhibition and her father got to hear of it and stopped it. Then she had a nervous breakdown and had to be taken away from her father. She went to stay with an aunt in Asturias and then she married some military man and I don't think she's painted since."

Maria wondered if he had been in love with her. " Did you know her well ? "

" Quite." He took her arm and led her over to a bench. " Let's sit here and look at the factories if you don't like swans."

They sat down in silence and she scratched at the gravel with her foot. After that girl she must seem very tame stuff to him. " Tell me more about her," she said at last. " She sounds so interesting. I suppose you don't see her now."

" No. Her father still lives here, but she doesn't often come to see him. The last time I heard from her was when she was in Asturias. She wrote wonderful letters with illustrations right across the page covering the writing."

" I'd thought of writing to you from England," said Maria, " but my letters aren't very exciting and I never do illustrations."

She could have kicked herself for saying that, and wanted to say something cheerful quickly to shut out the wailing sound of her last words, but she could think of nothing. She tried to look casual by raising her eyebrows and drew a large face on the ground with the toe of her shoe.

He watched her toe and when she had finished added a spiral top knot.

As they walked back to her tram stop, he mentioned that he would be away in Tolosa all the next day. He had to take his family car to be mended, they always took it there, to a man who had once been their chauffeur.

She almost believed he had made it up on the spur of the moment, because he was fed up with her. When he took her arm to guide her across the road she pulled it away from him.

She made no reply to his final Goodbye and climbed into the tram without even looking at him.

8

When she arrived home she felt furious with everyone and had no appetite for supper. Miss Pearson disapproved of her lack of appetite almost as much as of her " running around with a Spaniard." " Well, dear," she said, for she always called her " dear " when she was annoyed, " did you have a nice time with your painter friend ? "

" Yes, thank you."

" We listened to the radio and heard such a lovely broadcast from England, didn't we, Ethel ? "

" I didn't know they broadcast anything except religious services from England on Sunday afternoons," said Maria.

" Oh yes they do," Miss Pearson quivered with suppressed anger, but she spoke triumphantly as though they, too, went in for the most up-to-date gaiety. " Why, we listened into jazz ! "

" Everyone doesn't find religious services dull," said Ethel, who was older and plainer than Maria and, therefore, always sided against her.

" I don't like jazz," said Maria, priggishly, " and I should have thought that being a Catholic you wouldn't want to listen to a Protestant service."

This was too much for Miss Pearson. " I have a respect for
every religion . . . and I'd like to know how you, who don't
even go to Mass on Sundays, can sit there dictating to us."
Her purple turkey's neck seemed about to burst the band of
silvery beads mounted on satin which held it back.

Maria's depression made her quarrelsome. " How's the headache ? " she asked Ethel, knowing that nothing irritated Miss
Pearson more than to have the subject changed.

" Better, thank you," said Ethel, stiffly.

Miss Pearson was determined to have her say. " It's no
wonder she has a headache. Anyone would who's responsible
for you," and she dwelt on Maria's flightiness, rudeness and
ingratitude.

" Well, I'm glad her headache is better now," said Maria.
" It may not be my ingratitude, it may be her diet."

" The food in this house is as good as you'd get anywhere.
I'm very particular what we eat." This was true, the food was
delicious, and one of the reasons why Maria had not walked out.

" I never said anything against it. It agrees with me all right.
I never get headaches, but some people feel better on very little
nourishment, just orange juice and salads. Ethel's always
eating."

" I am *not*," said Ethel.

" Well, anyhow, it's unfair to me to let what I do give you
headaches."

After supper, the other two played cards, while Maria looked
out of the window on to the beach. It was pouring with rain
and the sea was greenish grey and rough. Why had Alonso
mentioned this wretched girl ? Why had he made no reply when
she suggested writing to him ? Why on earth had she suggested
it, anyhow ? It was always she who made the suggestions, who
asked him questions. He never bothered, he probably just found
her a flattering audience. He hadn't arranged to meet her again.
Perhaps it was because he thought she was engaged to Manolo.
This consoled her. " It isn't that I'm in love with him," she
decided, " but I want him to fall in love with me." It was no
use brooding about it, but she couldn't help it.

" You always have the luck," Miss Pearson was saying to

Ethel. " I don't see how I'm to win now."

" Well, it doesn't really matter in this game," said Ethel. It was double patience. " It's nice to win, but the thing is to get it out."

" You ought to speak Spanish to me while we're playing, otherwise you'll never learn."

" I know, but I'm so bad about picking up languages and I can't get a good accent."

" You shouldn't worry about your accent. That's nonsense. One doesn't want to speak like a Spaniard. I remember Señora de Urquijo always said it was so pretty to hear Spanish spoken with an English accent." She had certainly kept her English accent intact. " It's better not to have a good accent if you don't mind how you get it."

Maria felt suddenly uneasy and wondered if Miss Pearson had overheard the fruity conversations of Señor Jaime Torre. Surely not, or she'd have said something about it before now. She must be referring to going out with Manolo and Alonso. All the same it gave her a nasty turn and made her want to be safely back in favour. With a diffident air she turned to Miss Pearson. " Would you tell my fortune, please—when you've finished your game, of course ? "

" You know I never tell fortunes on Sunday." Miss Pearson was delighted to be able to refuse her something and triumphed for a short time, but, being a kind woman as long as she was treated like a benefactress, she soon melted. " You may play rummy with us in a few minutes."

Miss Pearson won the first round and this put her in a good temper. " I'm quite lucky tonight," she said. " I won the last game and I'd never have imagined I should, but Ethel got stuck for a long time and I pulled up. I had the most extraordinary cards. Sometimes I'm unlucky and then I'm very lucky. Did I ever tell you how I won the gordo in the loteria of Navidad ? " While priding herself on having retained her native accent, when she spoke Spanish, she used Spanish words frequently when she spoke English.

" No," said Ethel, untruthfully.

Maria thought being nice could be carried too far. " Yes,

you did tell us. The man did you out of the money, though, didn't he ? "

" Yes, I'm sure he must have done, because soon after he opened a new shop, much larger than the estanco he'd had before. I often regret not putting my name on the back of my ticket. People can be so mean. And I was so silly, ' Leave the ticket with me, Señora, and I'll see if its the right one,' and I did, but I said, ' Of course, it's the right one, I've seen the number in the papers,' ' Sometimes there's a difficulty about it and they make mistakes,' he said, and I left the ticket with him and when I went back he simply said I must have made a mistake about the number."

Miss Pearson was very kind and very wilful. To have been a governess and companion to Spanish aristocrats might have crushed someone weaker, but she had emerged self-assured and autocratic. She had never been servile or pandered to her employers, on the contrary she had ruled them with a rod of iron, not only the children but the parents as well. They had bequeathed her a nice little income, but she was absolutely unmercenary and had no idea of money. She had been swindled right and left when she sold the furniture, books and pictures in the legacy. Now, in her little flat, she behaved as though she was still in the old house. She was generous and, though Ethel and Maria paid a small sum for their keep, she can have made nothing out of it because she gave them wonderful meals with special treats on feast days, and many presents such as packets of cigarettes and sweets. When she was in a good mood she would tell Maria about her life in Spain, and make violent attacks on the behaviour of the aristocracy and the clergy, although she was on their side. She disapproved of the Jesuits.

Until Maria started going out with Manolo, Miss Pearson had treated her with great affection, and her present treatment was the result not only of authoritarianism but also of hurt feelings.

Half way through the second round, the phone bell rang. Mercedes, the cook, came in. " It's for Señorita Maria. A Señor," she said.

Miss Pearson frowned. Maria's heart beat, but she left the

room unhurriedly to show it could be nothing in which she was very interested.

It was Alonso's voice. " Have you got to give lessons as usual tomorrow ? "

" Yes, why ? "

" I was going to suggest you come with me to Tolosa. It's a nice trip and we could eat there, but if you've got lessons it's no good. We might not be back till after six."

" Oh, I might arrange something. What time do you want to go ? "

" About twelve."

" That gives me heaps of time to give one lesson in the morning and I can put the other off."

" Good. Well, meet me at twelve at the café. It's dull going alone. I say, won't the English ladies be angry if you're out all day ? "

" No, I don't think so. Goodbye."

She rang the fat boy's house at once and arranged that he should come early. It was best to present Miss Pearson with a *fait accompli*. She walked slowly back to the drawing room, determined to be tactful and calm.

" Well, who was it ? " snapped Miss Pearson.

" Alonso."

" And what did he want ? "

" He wanted me to go to Tolosa tomorrow."

" And what did you say ? "

" I said yes. I thought it would be interesting to go there."

" Nonsense, it's a very ugly place. *I* shouldn't want to go there. Are you going *alone* with him ? What about your lessons ? "

" I've arranged to give them both in the morning before I go, I may not be back till after tea."

" And what time are you starting, I'd like to know ? "

" About twelve."

" Do you mean to say you're going to be from twelve to six getting to Tolosa and back. Why, it's quite near. What are you going to do there, I should like to know ? "

" His car has to be mended there. You never know how long

these things may take."

"Fancy going all the way to Tolosa to get a car mended, when there are far better places here. What rubbish! I've never heard such nonsense."

"Well, there's a man there who always mends their car, and I suppose they like to give it to him."

Miss Pearson took a deep breath. "So you're going out to lunch. You're going to alter the time of your lessons. You're going off all day like that with a Spaniard! I'd thought that kind of thing was finished now. You must be out of your mind."

Maria tried to be conciliatory. "You see, it's my last week here and I'd like to see something of the country. . . ."

"I should have thought you'd have found out enough about the country with that other Spaniard of yours! My goodness! Out all day like that!"

9

The morning of the excursion to Tolosa was sunny and mild. Unlike the heat-wave days, when the weather settled down to an unrelenting, steady heat which only a thunderstorm could shake, this day was as soft and fresh as a fine day in Spring. After the rain of the previous days, the air smelt delicious, and the trees seemed a brighter green. Coming from the dark drawing room where she had been giving her lesson, Maria was enchanted by the clear, gentle light on the white buildings and the coloured tents of the beach. The reds, blues, yellows and greens glowed and the water was as smooth and shiny as syrup.

Alonso, late as usual, came on foot. He was looking sleepy, his eyes puffy, and though he was shaved, he looked as though he hadn't finished getting up.

"I must have a drink," he said.

"And where's the car ? "

"In Tolosa."

" But you said you were taking it there."

" Did I ? I can't have done. I'm going for it and we'll bring it back."

" I suppose we'll have to go by train." She was disappointed and knew how uncomfortable short distance trains could be.

After a glass of pernod, he became more benevolent. " The best thing to do is to take a taxi to the station and wait until a train comes. I've got a lot of money today. We can have drinks everywhere and travel first. That won't be so uncomfortable for you." He helped her up and took her arm as they walked to the taxi rank.

The thought of sitting in a taxi or train was delicious when her legs felt so unsteady. " The pernod's gone to my head. I didn't have any breakfast."

In the taxi she closed her eyes. Great balls of orange and yellow floated on a greenish background and the whole world seemed to be quivering.

Alonso was unusually energetic and competent. He helped her out of the taxi carefully, bought the tickets and found out about the train, led her tenderly to a bench in the sun and sat beside her, large and reassuring.

She fell fast asleep shortly after the train started and woke to find Alonso sitting in front of her looking out of the window. There was a smut on his cheek.

" Did I miss anything ? " she asked.

" Yes, beautiful Basque scenery, witches and Druids, hundreds of them." It was Manolo's voice.

" I'm tired of Basque scenery. Tell me about Castille. I've always wanted to go there."

" Perhaps you will. Perhaps I'll be there to show you round." He had never seemed so considerate, almost fatherly. " I've got a surprise for you," he said.

" What ? "

He said he'd tell her later, but gave her clues to hold her interest. He teased her about it and then told her to forget it. She looked out of the window. The sky had clouded over and the sun had disappeared.

" It'll probably rain," she said.

He laughed, leant forward and slowly took one of her hands and held it in both of his. " That's an English form of conversation. If you're not careful you'll grow up like those elderly ladies with big teeth who wear beige. They trot round Europe talking about the weather."

" If you go on telling me how awful I'll be when I'm older," she said, " it's going to inhibit me and I'll never be able to say anything."

" Poor Marichu! " It was the first time he had called her that, and although he was laughing at her, the pressure of his dry, warm hands was firm. He looked at her as though insisting that she should look at him and not out of the window.

Tolosa station was small, unsheltered and almost deserted. It was beginning to rain. There were neither buses, trams nor taxis and they had to walk to the garage which was some way away. He held her arm closely as they walked and told her a story to illustrate real elegance:

" A man once had a beautiful house in a lovely garden of which he was very fond. One day he went for a long walk and when he came back the house and garden had disappeared. ' If I ask people where it's gone,' he thought, ' it will seem absurd.' So he went to a psycho-analyst."

They were drenched by the time they reached the garage. It was a large, ramshackle shed with an office in the loft, to reach which they had to climb a rickety ladder. " A nice garage, isn't it ? " said Alonso.

A young lad with brown skin and flashing teeth told them the car was mended, but the lights wouldn't work. Having taken them up to the office and made them sit down to make his statements appear more businesslike, he said that he didn't know where the others were and he himself couldn't do anything until they came back.

" Will it be ready if we come back after lunch ? "

" Perhaps. I will do all I can, Señor."

He wrote down a number of particulars very slowly in a large book, looking up and smiling at them with pride from time to time.

Then they walked through the pouring rain, barely glancing

at the market place and old, narrow streets, until they found a café. Wet and depressed, they played ludo and looked at the torn, brilliantly coloured posters of bullfights round the walls. There was nothing particularly interesting about Tolosa at the best of times, but on a sunny day it might have been a pleasant place. The people who lived there appeared to be cut off from the outer world in spite of the radio and very old films at the local cinema. Very small provincial towns abroad on a rainy day seemed like the end of the world.

Leaving Maria in the café, Alonso went back to the garage before lunch to make sure they were doing something about the car. He was away a long time and when he returned he was very irritated. " The others aren't back yet and that boy doesn't know a thing. I've never come across such a place."

" Does your family always go there ? "

" Yes, the man's my father's foster brother."

In Spain many wealthy or well born women do not suckle their own children, but give them to a wet nurse who lives in the house, is fed like a turkey cock and wears a splendid uniform. Her children thus become the foster brothers and sisters of the child she suckles, and quite often they remain friendly throughout their lives, although they are of very different classes.

" And where is he ? " asked Maria.

" How do I know ? He's disappeared. They've all disappeared."

By the time they had lunch it was three o'clock. The proprietor of the café recommended a small restaurant and there they were given some thick bean soup, some chicken and a bottle of rough red wine. Alonso liked the restaurant with its many plants in brass pots, red plush and thick curtains, and said he would like to paint it. " This is a permanent fashion in small restaurants," he said, " and not of any particular date."

After lunch he left her once again in the café with the bull-fight posters and went back to the garage. When he came back, soaked through, he was in a really bad temper. The others had come and gone in his absence and nothing had been done about the lights. They probably hadn't even discussed them. " So there's nothing to do but wait here," he said, " unless you'd like to see a very old Spanish film."

The shrivelled little café proprietor who had been hovering near them (they were the only people there) interposed: " The cinema doesn't open till the evenings."

" Well, it'll have to be ludo, then. A walk is out of the question."

The game was silent and long. He refused to carry on a conversation. When it was over, he said, " Now tell me an enormously long story."

" I can't remember any now."

" Make one up."

" I can't."

He eyed her coldly. " Don't look so miserable."

" I'm *not* miserable. If I look it I don't feel it."

He launched into a long diatribe against the garage, the weather and Tolosa. She felt he would have liked to include her in it, too.

" Why don't you say something," he said at last.

" What shall I say ? "

" Why don't you try and cheer me up ? What's the use of being so clever ? What's the use of reading so much ? You can't even entertain me when there's nothing else to do."

" I didn't read so much," she said primly, " and I didn't become clever—if I am clever—in order to entertain you when you're having a fit of bad temper."

She picked up a paper from another table and forced herself to concentrate on it. It was local, and in it she learnt for the first time that trouble was brewing in the Basque provinces. A large strike was feared. Dissatisfaction with wages had reached a climax in the Asturias and Seville as well. The attitude of the Asturian miners was described as menacing.

There were a number of crimes. A woman had been found with her throat cut in a village of Navarre. A man had killed his father in a quarrel. A Basque labourer had stolen a bicycle. An attempt had been made on the life of a prominent right wing official when he was returning from the funeral of his friend who had been murdered a week before.

The funerals of people murdered for political reasons usually led to further violence, and she remembered the cortége she had seen in Calle Garibay where the mourners cast furious looks at a hostile crowd on the pavement. There had been at least four political murders that summer.

She turned to the announcements of weddings, two of them with photographs of the bridal party. She read the advertisements and the sports page with its long lists of pelota results. When she had read every part of the paper she looked through it again to see if she had missed anything.

" I'm going back to the garage for the last time." said Alonso. " If they haven't done the car by now, we'll take the next train back."

His temper was worse when he returned. " We'll go to the station now. I can't stand another minute of this wretched place." She felt he might start hurling insults at her at any moment and, angry as she was, decided to give him no opening.

After a long, damp, silent wait under the only available shelter in the station, she found herself once more in a first class compartment, but this time shivering with cold, her wet hair dripping on to her shoulders. She had come out in a thin linen suit, quite unsuited to this weather. There was a smell of damp clothes and the raindrops streamed down the window panes.

She looked through the slanting lines of rain at the landscape beyond. That had become familiar several weeks ago. It was everything Manolo said it was, except mysterious. The small hills, the valleys with their clusters of simple buildings, needed no explanation or legend.

The train kept stopping for no apparent reason. Alonso slept or pretended to sleep.

At the end of the journey she said, firmly, " Thank you for the excursion. I must go straight home now and change my things."

Alonso was taken aback. " Please don't go home."

" I shall catch cold if I don't."

" Well, let me take you there in a taxi."

In the taxi he pleaded with her to change her mind. He said he would wait for her outside while she went up to the flat.

" Once I'm up there, I can't very well come out again. I had quite enough trouble with them about going to Tolosa as it is."

When they had nearly reached Ondarreta, without consulting her he asked the taxi to turn back and take them to Sacha. " We'll go there," he said, disarmingly, " because that's where I first met you. You'll soon get warm and dry there."

" I shall catch a cold."

" Marichu, darling, please! "

In Sacha he ordered hot coffee and sat beside her on the upholstered seat. " You're angry," he said, " You hate me. It was a horrible excursion. You never want to go out with me again." His opaque, black eyes stared at her face with a melancholy expression.

" Honestly, I can't think why you asked me."

" Because otherwise I shouldn't have seen you today. I'm not used to taking girls out and I do everything wrong." He took her hand and when she tried to pull it away held it firmly. " Let me tell you about my surprise."

" Alright."

" Well, I shall make the portrait much better and then I want you to have it instead of sending it to Manolo. Please— you must agree."

" But Manolo's expecting it."

" Oh, never mind. You must take it back to England with you. It'll be a souvenir of me. When you see it you'll think— Alonso must be drinking in some café at this moment."

She said she would think it over. He bought three large packets of English cigarettes for her, and said he would like to go round the shops with her and buy her anything she wanted.

She laughed, " It's the wrong sort of weather for that."

He persuaded her to go to a film. In the street he took her arm. His height and bulk loomed magnificently beside her, seeming to shower down affection from above.

In the cinema a Polar expedition was showing to the accompaniment of very high chords. They had a small box to themselves near the back. He stared at her so fixedly that she was almost uncomfortable. Then he kissed her hand, put his arm round her shoulders and kissed her cheek.

10

If there was one thing Maria loathed it was getting up in the morning. At eight a bad tempered Mercedes would bang loudly and repeatedly on the door, and when all had been called she would sing out of tune at the top of her voice or scream an angry monologue at the cat, Pomti Pom, while she cleaned the passage, to make sure no one went to sleep again. Some time between eight and half-past she would dump the breakfast in the dining room (which was not a room at all but part of a large entrance hall and, therefore, cold and draughty) without telling anyone, and by the time Maria arrived, the coffee was usually cold. Miss Pearson breakfasted in bed.

This morning, however, Maria was dressed early. She woke at six and lay looking at the stripe of light between the curtains, feeling happy and triumphant as she thought of the events of the day before. Alonso must be very attached to her. He would probably tell her so today, that was all that mattered. She didn't know what she felt about him, it was of no importance really.

She answered Mercedes' irritating knock by appearing at the door fully dressed and saying, " There's no need to go on knocking. I'm up."

On her way to the dining room she stroked the skinny Pomti Pom and tried to get the two canaries to sing. She was delighted to drink her coffee hot for a change. When her cousin appeared she greeted her warmly and inquired about her headache, poured out her coffee for her and handed her everything she could possibly want. She tried to imagine what it was like to be Ethel.

" When you have a headache, Ethel," she said, " do you find you want people to realise what it's like for you to have a head-ache, or do you just want them to be nice and fetch you things and look after you without realising what your headache's like ? "

Ethel was bewildered and had no taste for these discussions of Maria's. " I don't quite see what you mean. I don't like to be a bother to anyone and I'm always grateful for anything people do for me."

" That'll be the second thing."

Miss Pearson arrived, carrying her tray, clad in her mauve dressing gown. She was very flustered. " There's one of those strikes on," she said. " Good morning, Ethel. Good morning, Maria. One of those strikes they keep on having."

" Good morning, Miss Pearson," they said together. It was a fatal mistake to forget to say good morning, whatever the circumstances might be. It was the same with good night.

It was most unusual to see her at this hour. Her grey hair was rolled in curlers and tucked away under a pale, blue net which emphasised the beakiness of her great nose. " Poor Mercedes couldn't get a tram—she had to walk all the way to the market and back. It doesn't do anyone any good—this kind of thing . . . and for all their socialist talk," she looked at Maria sternly, " it's the poor people who come out of it the worst." She sat down.

" Can I pour you out some more coffee ? " said Maria, still full of goodwill.

Miss Pearson nodded permission. " The rich have cars and taxis," she went on, " it doesn't matter to them about the strike. It's the poor who have to walk when there aren't any buses."

" Some of the rich, the people who *own* the buses and trams, don't come out of it so well," said Maria, persuasively.

" Well, dear, whatever you think, *I* think it's very mean of a few men, just because they want more money—and I'm sure they'd get it if they were patient and went the right way about it—it's very mean of them to refuse to work when they know how it affects those poor people going to work, sometimes carrying heavy things."

" Is it just a bus and tram strike, then ? "

" I don't know. But the buses and trams are certainly in it. They're always the first to do these things."

Mercedes came in with more rolls and butter. Miss Pearson looked up at her like some furious purple bird and began to question her in Spanish. " What kind of a strike is it ? "

" *Everything's* shut, Señora," Mercedes' eyes lit up. She was not a revolutionary, but she enjoyed a strike almost as much as a row with Miss Pearson. " Yes," she continued, trying to alarm them more and more " you can't go out you know. It isn't safe. All the strikers are walking about. They're sending out the Guardia Civil. There'll be shooting. There's trouble in the South and Asturias, too. It may be revolution. There'll be a lot of shooting before it's over! "

" They're always doing that kind of thing in this country," said Miss Pearson. " These huelgas! Ever since the King's gone, there's been trouble. They'll be going on bended knees and asking him to come back one of these days."

" What's the strike about ? " Maria asked Mercedes.

" Money, Señorita " said Mercedes, grinning, " money," and she twiddled an imaginary coin between her thumb and finger.

" Where's the local paper ? "

" It didn't come."

" That shows things are as bad as can be," said Miss Pearson. " Well, we can't go out today. None of us."

This was a blow. Maria protested, " But I must give my lesson."

" Nonsense. You can't go. It's not safe. There's always shooting," said Miss Pearson. " No one in their senses would dream of going out with all these angry workmen in the streets. They're very dangerous."

" I'm sure it isn't dangerous. My pupils will be expecting me."

The argument went on. Miss Pearson was determined that Maria should not go out, she really believed she might be shot. Maria's only concern was to see Alonso.

After breakfast she phoned her pupils and found to her disgust that they wouldn't hear of her coming for the lesson. The duchess's son, too, would not be coming that day, although he only lived two streets away.

Miss Pearson dressed quickly and appeared in the drawing room, ready for any emergency. Ethel was told to phone the British Consul.

" It may be necessary to hang out the Union Jack," said Miss Pearson, " Who knows what will happen ? "

Ethel came in and announced that the Consul's secretary said it might be serious. It seemed to Maria that they were all being over-dramatic. Miss Pearson held forth about the political situation at great length. It was all because the Monarchy had gone. In the days of Primo de Rivera there had been law and order and soup kitchens for the poor.

" Free soup isn't everything," said Maria.

Miss Pearson continued. In the days of the Monarchy there had been no strikes.

" There was a revolution," said Maria.

Miss Pearson became indignant. " The King needn't have gone if he didn't want to. He abdicated to avoid bloodshed. You know very well he did."

" He knew whose blood it would be."

They heard the telephone ringing and Mercedes hurrying to answer it.

" Well, the telephone wires haven't been cut yet," said Miss Pearson. " They stop at nothing, you know."

" How can they cut the wires unless they storm the telephone building ? "

It was Señor Jaime Torre on the phone. He wanted to come and give a lesson in spite of everything, because he lived so near. He was opposed to the strikers on political grounds, and he was also annoyed at the prospect of being cooped up with his two pupils all day, with no young women in the house and no one to discuss love and women with. He told Maria she could take it from him the strike wouldn't last more than a day or two. Something of the sort had been expected and they were prepared for it. If necessary it would be put down by the military, but the Guardia Civil should be able to cope with it.

Maria thought it better that he shouldn't come for a lesson.

" I told him it was too dangerous," she told Miss Pearson. " He thought it would be all right as I was so near, but I persuaded him not to come."

Miss Pearson was pleased. She disliked Torre and thought he was laughing at her when he bowed over her hand gallantly, complimenting her on her charming flat and excellent Spanish, on those occasions when he met her in the passage. " That was quite right."

Ethel started a crossword. Miss Pearson took up some

needlework and Maria tried to read. The silence was broken
only by the tick of a small, gilt clock, the heavy breathing of
Miss Pearson and Ethel's sighs.

After a time, Maria went out on to the balcony, although it
was raining slightly. There were a number of people in the
street who stood in groups talking and gesticulating. The beach
was deserted. Not a single tent was up. There was no sound of
rioting. She came in. "Everything looks just the same as usual,
except that there aren't any buses or trams. There are people
walking about, girls and women, too. It can't be very dangerous."

"I heard a shot," said Miss Pearson.

"So did I," said Ethel.

"I haven't heard anything," said Maria. "It might have
been a door banging downstairs. Anything sounds like a shot if
you're trying to hear one."

The next disturbance was caused by the cigarette situation.
Both Maria and Ethel smoked a great deal. In spite of the
ruinous price of English cigarettes, they kept to those and only
smoked the sweet, black canarias when they could get nothing
else.

"Have you got any cigarettes?" said Ethel.

"About six." Of the three packets which Alonso had bought
for her in Sacha, she had only brought home one, because he
had absent-mindedly put the other two in his pocket.

"They won't last long," said Ethel.

"If Alonso phones, I could ask him to bring some round.
He usually has a supply."

"You'll do nothing of the sort," said Miss Pearson. "Perhaps
after lunch, Mercedes will go and get some."

"The estancos may be shut and they only have canarias
round here."

Late in the morning Alonso phoned. "There won't be any
sitting today, will there?" he said, sadly. "How are we going
to meet?"

"I don't know. I'm fed up with this strike."

"I thought you were all for them."

"Well, I am, but —"

"You're as bad as the rest of us!"

" I've been defending the strikers all the morning, but it's so miserable. I can't go out and we haven't any cigarettes."

" I could bring you some. I've still got those two packets I meant for you."

" But isn't it dangerous ? I wonder if you should." She thought for a moment. " Hold the line. . . ."

She hurried back to the drawing room. " You see, Miss Pearson, he's offered to bring some cigarettes. I didn't ask him. He simply offered because he happened to ask how we were off for cigarettes. What shall I say ? He doesn't think it dangerous. People often exaggerate, you know." She had a brilliant idea. ' *You* talk to him, Miss Pearson. I'm sure *you'll* be able to judge whether it's dangerous or not."

Miss Pearson couldn't resist the temptation to interfere in someone else's phone conversation. She looked as though she were doing a great favour. " Very well, I'll talk to him."

Maria walked about the room in suspense. How would Alonso talk to Miss Pearson ? Would he be tactful ? Anyhow, if he didn't come, it was something to know that he wanted to see her so much.

Miss Pearson returned, bustling and important. " He's coming over later in the day *if* things are quieter. He'll make quite sure things are all right first. I insisted on that. It looks much better coming from me."

" Yes it does," said Maria, " much better."

11

Alonso arrived just before lunch, out of breath. He was very tidy in a dark blue suit. Mercedes was in the kitchen, so Maria answered the door. He looked round very carefully and then gave her a quiet kiss. " Your lift isn't working," he said. He lowered his voice: " I want to meet the charming lady I talked

B

to over the phone.   She sounds delicious."

" You must be very careful with her."

He was. He entered the drawing room firmly and quietly, and made an excellent impression by handing the two packets of cigarettes to Miss Pearson instead of giving them to Maria. He shook hands respectfully, but did not make the mistake of Jaime Torre by bowing low, and addressed himself to Miss Pearson as though she were the person he had really come to see. He was also very courteous to Ethel.

" I hope you didn't have any difficulty in coming," said Miss Pearson.

" Oh no, it's quite quiet round here. What a pretty flat you have! " His tone was exactly right, convincing and not gushing.

" Do you think so ? I haven't troubled about it much."

Unostentatiously, he bent down and stroked the thin, large, white Pomti Pom, which had come to rub itself against his leg. " What a lovely cat, so thin! I like cats to be bony, they look more graceful."

" He's a bit too thin," Miss Pearson beamed, " though he eats an enormous amount."   She had been expecting to see someone with long hair and wild eyes, and was very relieved by Alonso's plump, solid, bourgeois appearance. The dark suit put years on him.

" What do you call him ? " he said.

" Pomti Pom. There was a little song, you know, in England, that we used to hear a lot at one time. ' Oh what did I do with my umbrella ? Pomti Pom.' "

Alonso laughed immoderately at this. He began by chuckling and then worked himself up until he was shaking all over. Maria noted with surprise that this was not put on, but then she remembered how several jokes which were pointless and flat for her had a strange exotic charm for him. Miss Pearson, who had been ready to suspect Alonso of trying to get round her could not doubt his response, and was delighted to see her joke go down so well.

" How long do you think the strike will last ? " she said.

" I don't know. I hope it ends soon."

" That's not like Maria. I'm sure she wants it to get worse.

She'd like a revolution."

He laughed. " It may last for a few days, but I don't think it'll be serious." He turned to Ethel so that she should not feel excluded from the conversation. In an extraordinary accent he explained, " Very sorry. I not speak English."

" It's quite all right," said Ethel, " I can understand. It's good for me to hear Spanish."

" There's a much worse strike in Asturias," he went on, " and in the South. It's more like a rising there."

" I hope they put an end to it soon."

" I've no doubt they will. There was going to be a general rising in various parts, but already it's fizzled out in some places, and I don't think it will come to anything here. It was badly organised."

" Really ? My goodness ! " said Miss Pearson. " And where's the worst in San Sebastian ? "

" Round the port, in the Avenida, the Bulevar and near the Kursaal."

" Did you see anything on your way here ? We heard a shot."

" No, everything's all right round here for the moment. The Antiguo's pretty safe. Anyway, the strikers aren't doing anything, but the Guardia Civil has orders to shoot if they see more than five people together. Of course, they only shoot in the air to scare them, but a stray bullet might get someone."

" Oh, how awful," said Maria, tired of being left out of it. " That seems quite unnecessary. Has anyone been killed ? "

" I think one or two people were wounded near the port."

" I think it's awful to fire on people who haven't any arms."

" They were doing their duty," said Miss Pearson.

" The men were trying to overturn a lorry," said Alonso.

" A blackleg lorry, I suppose," said Maria.

" I'm not so sure that they haven't arms," said Alonso.

" I'm sure they have," said Miss Pearson.

" I hope they have and I wish they had more," said Maria.

Now she was annoyed with Alonso. He couldn't simply be playing up to Miss Pearson. He didn't care about anything. He didn't mind how many people were shot. He wasn't on either side.

" And how do you like San Sebastian ? " said Alonso to Miss
Pearson. " You must know it better than I do, of course. I hear
you've lived in Spain a long time. One can see that by the way
you talk."

Miss Pearson admitted she knew Spain very well. She gave
the name of her former employer and they discovered that a
distant relation of his had married a cousin of Alonso's. She
was delighted to find him so well connected.

When Mercedes came in to say lunch was ready, Miss
Pearson was most reluctant to stop the conversation. She was
comparing lists of names with Alonso and going into family
trees.

" And so you know the Urquijos ? " she said.

" I painted Doña Carmen."

A person who painted the portraits of these exalted personages
was quite different from a painter. Miss Pearson was warmed
up to indiscretion. " I never got on with her myself."

" She is rather difficult."

At last lunch could be kept waiting no longer. Miss Pearson
rose. Alonso opened the door for her and said he was sorry to
go now, but he couldn't keep them from their lunch. He hoped
he might pay them another visit and would be delighted to
bring them cigarettes or anything else they needed. He said
goodbye to Maria less respectfully than to the others, but in the
same social tone.

12

The next day the situation had become worse and the reports
from other parts of Spain were alarming. Mercedes came back
from market with many wild rumours and passed them on to
the others. Miss Pearson spent the morning phoning a number

of retired English teachers and governesses to find out what they thought. Because they had all heard several times how worried the doctors were about her heart, they assured her everything was all right and there was nothing to worry about, and, in any case, the English would be protected by their Consul. She refused to be reassured, rang up the Consulate, and was told once more that there was no cause for alarm.

Alonso rang up and asked to speak to Miss Pearson. After a long talk about the situation he asked her permission to take Maria for a walk, and having obtained it, did not even suggest speaking to Maria herself.

By lunch time she was sorry she had given permission. " I'm sure it's far too dangerous," she kept repeating.

" He wouldn't go if it's too dangerous," said Maria.

" He assured me he wouldn't," said Miss Pearson, " but he might not know. He might make a mistake."

" It's unhealthy staying in all day like this," said Maria. " A walk would do me good." She was tired of every single piece of furniture in the flat by now. " It's depressing! "

" What's depressing ? " asked Miss Pearson, sharply.

" Oh, the strike."

Before she retired for the siesta, Miss Pearson made Maria promise that she wouldn't go out unless Alonso was quite, quite certain there was no danger.

By the time he arrived, the others were fast asleep. The door bell rang shrilly and Maria hurried to answer it on tiptoe, afraid that the sleepers might be disturbed and come out and start interfering. " We must go at once. If we stay here we'll have to whisper all the time."

He nodded, gave her a wink and they hurried down three flights of stairs before they felt they could talk freely.

" I hope it's safe. They say it's worse," she said.

" Well, it's the second day. If a strike isn't over at once, everyone says it's getting worse." He had decided that they would go up the narrow path beside the church, it was unlikely that anything would be going on up there.

Two Guardias de Asalto, armed with rifles, lolling against the wall of the church, frowned at them. " Why are they looking at us like that ? " she asked.

He hailed them and shouted, " Is there anything going on up there ? Is it all right ? "

" Yes," said one of the men returning the smile, " but you'd better be back before it gets dark. We've got orders to shoot then."

" And they'd have let us go up without saying anything," she said. " It seems very cold blooded."

" They get so elated when there's a strike on, they don't know what they're saying." He explained that the Guardia de Asalto was very much to the left of the Guardia Civil, and might very well refuse to fire on the strikers.

The path was steep and uneven and they were forced to walk in single file. At the top there were fewer houses and some open fields looking down over the Antiguo and part of the bay. A breeze ruffled the trees, but no sounds came from the town of shouting or shooting. A grassy bank shone invitingly in the sun and they sat down there.

Alonso said he was glad to have seen the flat and enjoyed his meeting with Miss Pearson.

" I thought at first you were playing up to her," said Maria, but I believe you were being quite natural,"

" I'm going to do a sketch of Pomti Pom."

" That'll be *amusing* for you."

" Don't be angry. You know I do it so that I can come and see you."

" Yes, but you enjoy it, too. You enjoy everything as a kind of music hall turn."

" Ah, but I take *you* seriously, as seriously as anything."

" No you don't."

" Oh yes I do. I wish we'd been children together. You must have been a very serious little girl, with your fingers covered in ink."

" You must always have been smug and self-satisfied."

" Still, we would have got on very well."

" Oh well, what does it matter now ? "

He laughed. " You've no interest in the past, only in the future."

" The future's awful. I'm going in three days." If she had thought this would lead to some sort of declaration she was disappointed. He said nothing. She changed the subject. " I wish I knew a bit more about the strike and I wish you took it a bit more seriously."

" Why should I ? You're always lecturing me about not being serious. You tell me strikes are serious. I daresay they are. But do you ever read anything about the political situation in Spain ? No."

" Neither do you."

" But then I don't claim to be one of the serious ones. Have you ever bothered to find out how all this started ? No. You just say it's serious. Sometimes you say you wish you knew more about it. . . ."

" Well, how could I ? They don't know anything in the flat. Jaime Torre's a Fascist. The newspapers are all reactionary. Manolo's a funny sort of anarchist. That's the trouble."

" That's not the trouble at all. The trouble is that you're not really serious and you're dishonest about it. You won't admit what your real interests are at the moment: falling in love, being attractive, looking nice, new clothes, and so on."

She tried to interrupt but he went on, firmly. " Perhaps in time you really will enquire into the causes and effects of what goes on, whereas I shall always be content to react to events as they come. And in the end you won't like me, because, of course, it's the nature and privilege of the serious to be less tolerant than the others. But for the moment anyhow the difference between us isn't that you're serious and I'm not, as you suggest, but that I know what I am and you don't know what you are. So that when you accuse me of being facetious about the strike and when you are indignant because I enjoy Miss Pearson, it's difficult to argue with you because I'm arguing with a muddle. You don't seem to know the difference between taste and ethics. I only deal in the first." He looked at the ground with a sad stare. " I see no reason why I should make myself feel any more than I do. I don't really care about anything. It may be a limitation, but there you are."

" I don't mean to be ethical," she said, " I only am because

I don't know enough. I mean, I can't help feeling it's wrong to persecute the Jews and kill people. I should prefer to dislike it because it's stupid or unnecessary—but I have to think it's wrong. Don't you ? "

He shrugged his shoulders. " It's no use asking me things like that. Now I'll put some questions to you. Tell me, honestly, which would upset you most—to wake up covered in spots with all your hair falling out, or to hear the strike had been stamped out with the utmost ruthlessness ? "

" I shall never have to ask myself questions like that. It's not fair."

" Ah, but you must answer! *I* needn't because only the serious ones have to."

" All the same, I *do* care about the strike. You *can't* prove to me that I don't."

He saw she looked unhappy. " What's the matter Marichu ? Tell me. Did I say something which upset you ? What was it ? "

" Well, if you really want to know—it's your not caring very much about anything. I suppose you don't care nearly as much about me as I'd imagined since Tolosa."

" I do care about you, Marichu, really I do. It seems a lot to me, although it might not be much compared with what other people feel."

" Why do you come and see me every day ? " She meant to be calm and spoke very quietly. " Why do you behave as though you wanted to see me so much ? Why did you bring me those cigarettes and go for a walk with me ? "

" But I do want to see you every day. There's nothing I like more. You must know I do. I have a tremendous affection for you. It's nostalgic. I feel as though thousands of secrets and confidences are piled up behind us which we've never made. You think swans are badly balanced, you don't like relics of the monarchy, you are always furious about something. Now, if we had been children together it would be all right—it would be fixed—but now you're going away and who knows what'll happen when you're back in England ? But you're in the better position you know."

" I don't see how."

" You're young and you'll develop and keep changing. I'm something fixed. Nothing will ever alter me."

13

The next day Alonso arrived an hour before tea and began the sketch of Pomti Pom. There was no possibility of a walk now. The strike showed no signs of coming to an end, and there was more shooting. The Antiguo was no longer safe. There were grim reports from Oviedo and regiments were being sent there from Madrid. The hated "tercios," the Spanish Foreign Legion, which included a large number of Moors, were on their way there now.

Alonso told Maria as much as he knew about the situation in a very detached way which annoyed her. He found it impossible to go on with the sketch and cope with her irritation at the same time, and finally laid down his pencil and paper. " Well, don't let's talk about the strike any more," he said. " Please don't talk about it any more. You get so angry with me. Anyone would think I was the Government. If I tell you the miners in Oviedo are bound to be crushed, it isn't necessarily because I want them to be. Anybody can see that a few miners can't hold out against tanks and regiments, whether they're in the right or not."

" It's the way you say it—as though you were talking about the weather or something."

" I can see very well I shall have to talk an octave lower or in a hushed whisper every time I mention the strike."

The sketch of Pomti Pom advanced quickly. It was an easy cat to draw, not an indefinite mass of fur like most cats, because its bones gave it shape. Maria had come over to Alonso's point of view that it was a graceful animal, like an Egyptian cat, and she liked the drawing. She said she thought it much better than

B*

her portrait, and he explained to her that he was a skilled draughtsman and his sketches were always better than his oil paintings, because he always tired of anything which took a long time to finish. He'd never really finished a big picture properly in his life.

They were interrupted by the phone ringing, and Maria had to go and answer it because the others were still resting and would not be up until tea time. Alonso had graciously been invited to stay to tea because Maria, with a few carefully dropped hints, had let Miss Pearson guess that he was going to make her a present of the drawing.

It was Jaime Torre on the phone. He phoned twice a day and was more furious with the strike each time. There was no knowing when he would phone, because he had to wait until he had the phone to himself, so as not to be overheard telling Maria how awful his pupils were and how much he hated being a tutor.

Maria was rather pleased that he should have phoned while Alonso was there, and announced, wearily, when she came back to the drawing room, " It was Jaime Torre again. He's always phoning."

" Ah, those Andalusians! " laughed Alonso, who had heard all about him and thought him a joke.

" He hates the strike so much."

" Poor Señor Torre."

She knelt on the sofa beside him and looked over his shoulder.

" I'll put a lot of shading in it," he said. " That'll impress them. It'll look as though a lot of work's gone into it."

" Yes, they like things with a lot of work in them. They like a lot of detail, too. If you could sketch in part of the chair with the pattern and everything, they'd love that."

The room was full of photographs. On one wall there were a number of pictures of Miss Pearson's pupils and their parents, taken separately at different ages and in groups. They were a good looking family, all dark, small-featured and proud. Miss Pearson's two favourites, Concha and Maria Teresa, stood in silver frames on a table by themselves, smiling sweetly and mistily and swathed in gauze and roses, as was the fashion in photographs at the time. Above the sofa there was a large and imposing view of the family house, a great, white building standing in acres of its own parks somewhere near Granada. By themselves the pictures would have created a romantic idea of the family, but it was impossible for Maria to have that now after the innumerable anecdotes and descriptions given by Miss Pearson.

Alonso examined the photographs. " She must be a very nostalgic lady," he said. He looked at the two seascapes by the window very carefully and with obvious satisfaction. He told Maria how much he liked them, all of them, including the big coloured picture of Alfonso XIII, whom he referred to as " your Alfonsito," and the smaller one of the entire royal family. " Well, there's the whole of the English royal family in her bedroom," said Maria, sarcastically. " Why don't you ask her if you can see *them* ? "

He laughed, came over to the sofa, pulled her up and hugged her. " I'm not the conventional old stick you take me for," he said, " I'm going to abuse their confidence."

They heard a door shut at the end of the passage and she looked at him imploringly. " That's one of them. You must let me go."

" All right." He sat down quickly on the sofa and picked up his pencil and paper and she went to a chair near the door with a book.

" No, not a book," he whispered, " that's overdoing it. You're allowed to talk to me, I hope."

She laid the book down on the floor beside her and looked at the door. When Miss Pearson came in a little later she found him hard at work. He sprang to his feet and put the sketch down on the sofa where she couldn't see it. " It's not quite ready, you can't see it yet."

Miss Pearson smiled knowingly. " Oh no, I don't want to see it until it's finished." She turned to Maria. " Go and tell Ethel tea will be ready in five minutes."

When Maria returned, after giving a glowing account of the picture to Ethel while she did her hair, she found Miss Pearson in possession of the portrait of her darling cat, and Alonso about to leave. " But I thought you were staying to tea," she said.

" I've just been explaining to Miss Pearson that my mother may be worried about me and I ought to go home."

Maria was surprised, and Miss Pearson was glad to see he hadn't told Maria before and that he was so considerate to his mother. " I quite understand," she said.

" I'm so sorry I can't stay to tea, but I know you understand. Please give my regards to the other lady."

" And thank you very much for this," said Miss Pearson, " I'll hang it in my bedroom."

" That will be an honour! " He laughed so that Miss Pearson could see it was a joke she could share and not an absurd form of gallantry.

Maria accompanied him to the door, taking care to shut the drawing room door behind her. " But why aren't you staying ? "

" I couldn't face it at the last moment."

" But I thought you liked her."

" I love her, but if I get on with her, you disapprove of me, and if I don't it's awful for everyone. It's too difficult a situation for me to handle."

" Oh, you could handle anything."

" Not when you're mixed up in it, I couldn't." He kissed her good-bye.

This sudden change of mind was unlike him, and Maria sat puzzling over it during tea. Miss Pearson showed the picture to Ethel. " It's exactly like him," she said.

" Yes, perhaps not altogether," said Ethel, who was not so won over by Alonso, " but perhaps he does look like that sometimes."

" He looks exactly like that when he's sleeping," said Maria, " and you have to draw him sleeping, otherwise he isn't still."

" It's the only time you can draw him," said Miss Pearson, as though she had often tried. " It's very like him."

14

After tea, Ethel slipped off nobly and quietly to the Antiguo church to Benediction. She had received credit for this brave gesture in advance, in fact, since breakfast time. Maria and Miss Pearson played double patience, a new and elaborate form of it which Ethel had found in a book, and they had great difficulty in remembering the rules.

Miss Pearson had been seriously alarmed all day because they had heard several real shots, besides innumerable imaginary ones, and it had been very difficult to stop her from hanging out the Union Jack. In the end, Maria and Ethel had managed to convince her it wasn't necessary yet. There had been more and more phone calls to the British Consulate and the retired companions and English teachers to find out the dangers of the situation. They all said there was nothing to worry about, but Miss Pearson had set her heart on worrying and longed for an excuse to ransack the cupboards, find the old flag and hang it from the balcony.

" I don't think Ethel should have gone," said Miss Pearson.

" It's only across the road. Nothing much can happen in five yards' walk." Maria was tired of hearing how brave it was of Ethel. " There are always guardias round the church," she went on, coldly, " in fact, every time I look out of the window I see about six of them standing there, playing with their rifles. Ethel's certainly well protected."

Miss Pearson continued to be anxious. " I thought of sending Mercedes with her. Mercedes is good like that. She goes to the market and back every morning and won't stand any nonsense from anyone. Of course, she's *in* with these people."

There was a deep hostility mixed with mutual respect between Miss Pearson and Mercedes. Mercedes had been one of the maids at the Señora's summer residence in the old days, and when she left the Señora's service, Miss Pearson took her on. Every now and then they would have a scene, and Miss Pearson would decide that this time she really was going to give her a week's notice. The subject would be discussed endlessly at lunch and tea, and then by supper time it would all be over, and

Mercedes would go about her duties with a new willingness and good temper which lasted only a few hours.

Their game was interrupted by a wild-eyed Ethel, who rushed in, leaving the door open, and announced, " The most dreadful thing happened."

" Shut the door, Maria," said Miss Pearson, " it makes a draught."

They all sat down, Ethel and Miss Pearson on the sofa and Maria on the chair by the door. " Now tell us what it was," said Miss Pearson.

" It was after the Tantum Ergo," said Ethel, and paused. She was going to do justice to her story. " And what was so wonderful was that the priest had got up into the pulpit at the end of the first verse, but he waited there patiently and quietly until the singing was finished. Then he raised his hand and everyone was absolutely still, and he said, ' Before I tell you what I have to say, I want to ask each one of you to behave calmly and quietly. Remember, this is the house of God,' and then he paused. He didn't look alarmed or raise his voice. It was Father Ignacio . . ."

" Father Ignacio's a wonderful man," said Miss Pearson, " I like him far better than any of the others. I always enjoy his sermons."

" Which one is he ? " asked Maria.

No one answered, and Ethel continued: " I shall always remember how he behaved today. He said, ' Five bombs have been found outside the church. They are highly explosive. The Guardia Civil are seeing to them, but in case there should be any accident, I should like you all to leave the church at once in an orderly fashion.' Everyone went out in perfect order. I was amazed at how calm they were, although those bombs might have gone off at any moment." Ethel's voice was full of emotion and she shook her head slowly. " It was wonderful. Father Ignacio stood there in the pulpit not moving until everyone had gone. I was one of the last to leave, and as I went out of the door I saw he was still there, like . . . like the captain of a ship who waits till everyone has been rescued."

There was a respectful pause. Miss Pearson shook her head

in sympathy, and Maria coughed to clear her throat. " If the Antiguo was blown up," she said at last to ease the atmosphere, " some of the tower would be sure to fall on our balcony."

Miss Pearson and Ethel looked shocked. " If the Antiguo was blown up," said Miss Pearson, angrily, " you wouldn't get out of it so lightly. This piso would be smashed to pieces."

" The important thing," said Ethel, trying to recapture the tone of the conversation before Maria's remark, " is—that a church, a consecrated place—would be destroyed."

" Yes," said Miss Pearson.

" I don't see that there was much chance of it being blown up," said Maria, " if all the bombs had been found and the Guardia Civil was seeing to it."

" The bombs might go off accidentally, although the guardia was there," said Ethel, " and how do you know there weren't more bombs hidden somewhere else ? You always try and belittle everything. Just because it was a priest."

" Yes," said Miss Pearson, " just because it was a priest."

" If it was one of *her* friends who'd behaved like that, she'd think differently," Ethel went on.

" She would."

" I didn't say anything about the way he behaved. I don't remember mentioning him at all. I simply said there didn't seem to be much chance of the church being blown up, that's all."

" It isn't what you said," said Ethel, " it's what you implied. You always try and ridicule everything."

" Anyone can argue like that. You can just say the other person implied anything. I could say you implied my friends were cowards, but I don't."

" There, you've just said it."

" Don't argue with her," said Miss Pearson, " it's not worth it. She has no respect for anything or anyone." She turned her back on Maria, isolating herself with Ethel on the sofa, and went on as though there was no one else in the room. " How dreadful! How dreadful! There's nothing these people won't do. I wish you'd let me hang out that flag this morning. I shall certainly do so now."

" I don't think it would help," said Ethel, " I don't think it would protect the church."

" Oh yes it would. They wouldn't blow up anything so near a British flag. They know what they'd be up against there."

" You might lend the Union Jack to Father Ignacio to hang out of the church while you're about it," said Maria.

Miss Pearson turned round furiously. " How dare you say such a thing! How dare you make a mockery of the church! "

Maria didn't care any more. She was leaving in a day or two and they couldn't turn her out in the middle of a strike. " I wasn't making a mockery of anything. I think it's a good idea. Why don't you ? "

" Leave the room at once," said Miss Pearson, " I won't have you sitting there talking like that. *I won't have it*."

" All right," said Maria, shrugging her shoulders. She walked out of the room indolently with the smile on her face that Miss Pearson particularly detested.

15

Maria was not forgiven on Friday. Although it was her last day in the flat, the others were unwilling to talk to her, and she was forced to spend most of the morning alone in her bedroom. Ethel suggested to her, coldly, after breakfast that it might be the most tactful thing to do. She had to go to the drawing room to ask permission to phone her pupils.

" You may," said Miss Pearson, unrelentingly distant and not looking up from her needle work.

Maria phoned the two girls first and asked them to send the money they owed her to Miss Pearson as soon as they could. They were very nice, regretted not seeing her before she went, and insisted on paying her for the lesson she had been unable to give during the strike.

She then phoned up the pupil who had lessons only twice a week. This girl also insisted on paying her for the last week, had a long conversation about England and the strike, and unexpectedly asked Maria to write to her from London.

The Duchess was not so nice, in fact, almost angry that Maria had insisted on speaking to her in person. She was ready to make a fuss about the last four days.

" My other pupils are not deducting for this week," said Maria. " It seems to be the usual thing."

The Duchess yielded, not knowing how many pupils there were against her, nor who they might be.

Maria was forced to go to the drawing room again to discuss borrowing the money from Miss Pearson which her pupils would later refund. To avoid difficulties, she first wrote out the details of the plan in the form of a neat sum so that there was nothing to do but present it to Miss Pearson after the briefest exposition of the situation. Miss Pearson couldn't refuse to advance the money because if she did, Maria would have to stay until the strike was over. She looked at the piece of paper very closely, and then said, " Very well."

Jaime Torre phoned and Maria told him she was leaving the next morning.

" I am profoundly sorry not to see you again," he said. " My best wishes for your journey and future success with the Spanish classics."

He also told her that the strike would be over in a day or two. The worst was over now.

A little later, Alonso phoned to say his mother was so worried about him that he thought it better not to go out to-day.

" But you must," said Maria, " you must. I'm leaving to-morrow."

" Oh no."

" I've got to."

He insisted that she couldn't go without the portrait and it wasn't really finished yet. " Besides, it's in Gu."

" You'll have to post it on to me afterwards."

He knew a fisherman who lived near Gu and who might be able to get it to him in time. He promised to try to bring it with him in the afternoon. In any case he would come. " And how is dear Miss Pearson ? "

" Awful."

Maria was careful not to mention that he was coming at lunch time. The others would be in bed when he came, and he'd leave before they got up. If they saw the portrait they would know, but there was no reason why they should see it, and anyhow it didn't mattter about them knowing afterwards. She arranged with Alonso that he should tap quietly on the door instead of ringing the bell.

He arrived later than he had said, carrying a large parcel wrapped in newspaper under his arm. " It's the portrait," he said.

" I'm glad you could come, but it's a pity you came so late," said Maria. " You'll only be able to stay half an hour. You mustn't meet the others."

" Why not ? "

" They're so angry with me."

" Still ? " He laughed as though he couldn't believe it.

" They really are angry this time. I said she ought to lend Father Ignacio her Union Jack to protect the church."

" The English think we're very passionate," said Alonso, " but I've never met such strong feelings as there are in this flat."

They sat down together on the sofa and he picked up her hand. " I can't believe you're going to-morrow. You can't. There are no trains, no porters, no taxis."

" There are trains, and Miss Pearson's found a friend of Mercedes who'll take the luggage to the station. All her friends keep on telling her it's safe, they would even if it wasn't, because of her weak heart. Besides—the strike's practically over—Jaime Torre told me so."

" I'll join the strikers and get a band of them to stand menacingly outside your door."

" That won't be any good. She'll just wave a Union Jack at you."

He thought for a moment. " I know. I'll ring up this evening and talk to her. I'll tell her the situation's much worse and it's dangerous to move a step.

"She won't believe you."

"Are you going alone, unprotected, to the station?"

"I hadn't thought about that. Mercedes'll probably be sent with me."

He gave up trying to find a way out, and took out his packet of cheroots.

"You can't smoke one of those," said Maria, "they'd smell it. You must have one of my cigarettes."

He refused the cigarette and went over to the chair where he had left his parcel. He unwrapped it and disclosed not only the portrait but an oblong piece of painted metal. "Look," he said, "a surprise," and handed it to her.

She took it, found it unexpectedly heavy, and read the words: "Tram Stop—By Request." "What's this for?"

"A souvenir of the strike. I found it on the pavement. It's a thing one could only pick up during a strike—you wouldn't find one every day."

"No, you wouldn't."

"You could put it on your mantelpiece." He said "mantel-piece" in English. "One of the things I remember about England is the importance of mantelpieces. Everyone has one and puts important things on it."

"It's very heavy," said Maria, looking at it mistrustfully.

"Now, if you put it on your mantelpiece, think of the stories you can build round it. You'll be the only person in England with one of these. Think, Marichu." He took it from her and held it up. "The only person in England who has one. And I doubt if anyone in Spain has."

Maria could not tell whether he was serious or not. "I don't think there'll be room for it in my case."

"It won't take up any room. It's quite flat."

"But it's so heavy."

He put it down on the sofa and shrugged his shoulders. "Well, perhaps Miss Pearson would like it."

"I don't think so."

Disappointed, he turned her attention to the portrait. "Aren't you glad to have that?"

" Yes, very."

" Good."

Maria was silent for a minute. " This is the last time I shall
see you." She looked at him anxiously. " Will you miss me
when I go ? "

" Of course."

" Not very much, I suppose."

" Very much, as much as you like."

" How much ? " She put her arm on his shoulder.

" Do you want it in numbers, or what ? " He laughed and
got up from the sofa to prop the portrait against a chair where
they could both see it. " Do you like it any better ? "

" Yes, but not as a portrait, as a . . ., she fumbled for a word.

He walked across to the window. " It looks better from the
side."

" Perhaps it does." She didn't look.

" Much better. You'll have to hang it so that people get that
view of it."

She didn't answer, and looked despondently straight in front
of her, out of the window. She sighed.

Alonso did not return to the sofa, but moved slowly round
the room. It never ceased to fascinate him. " These roses are
wonderfully realistic," he said, referring to the roses painted by
a friend of Miss Pearson's on a small cupboard.

" I don't like them."

" I like the realistic approach to things of the English. The
first thing you see as you arrive in London are posters of huge
glasses of beer and biscuits, looking more like beer and biscuits
than one could possibly imagine. Are they still there ? "

" Yes."

He continued his examination of the roses. " Who did
these ? "

" Oh, some retired governess, I suppose."

" There must be hundreds of things covered with thickly
painted flowers by retired governesses."

" I suppose so."

He knelt down and looked at the roses more closely, rubbing
them gently with his finger.

" Do you realise we've only got a quarter of an hour left ? "
said Maria, sadly.

" Oh."

" After that I won't see you again for years. I may never see
you again in my life."

" Oh yes you will."

" How do you know ? "

" You're bound to come to San Sebastian again to see Miss
Pearson, aren't you ? "

" If I ever come to San Sebastian again, I shan't come near
this flat. I certainly shan't."

He was still looking at the roses.

" Oh, do stop looking at those horrible flowers," Maria burst
out. " It's simply affectation to like such things."

He stopped his examination of the drawing room and came
and sat beside her. She asked him what he would do when she
had gone, and he painted a picture of himself sitting dis-
consolately in cafés drinking innumerable pernods until it was
time to leave the North and go South to Madrid for the winter
with his family. He urged her to write to him and to come back
to San Sebastian the next year. He was obviously embarrassed
by partings, and was therefore refusing to treat this as one.
Nothing she could do would make him take the occasion
seriously.

At last, hearing a door bang in the passage, he seized the
opportunity and jumped to his feet. " There's one of them
coming, I must be off."

" They won't come in here."

" Perhaps I'd better go all the same." He picked up the
Tram Stop—By Request, saying, " I'll have to keep this
myself."

At the door he paused and said, " Remember, I dote on you.
And come back next year. And please come as far as the lift
with me."

They walked very quietly to the front door and she opened it
as noiselessly as possible. In the passage he gave her a final
hug " Phone me to-morrow," he said, " and if I'm asleep, tell
them to wake me. I'll try to be awake, though. You will phone,

won't you ? "

" All right."

" And remember, I'll miss you.   And I'll write to you."

He walked down three steps and looked back.   " Darling Marichu."

She smiled at him and went back into the flat.   Just as she had closed the door she heard a scratch on the other side.

Opening the grille, she saw Alonso.

" Don't forget to hide the portrait before they come," he whispered.

16

Maria slept very little during her last night in San Sebastian. She lay awake for a long time in the dark and then turned on the light and tried to read. At half-past four she fell asleep at last, but she woke up again twice after that.

It seemed to her that she had only just begun to sleep properly, when she was woken up by a dishevelled Mercedes with a nasty gleam in her eye, who shook the end of the bed and flung back the curtains as though she wanted the suddenness of the light to hurt Maria's eyes as much as possible. Maria cursed herself for having forgotten to lock her door. She felt sure that Miss Pearson had given Mercedes the fullest and most subtle instructions for waking her up as painfully as possible. She took a useless revenge by lying in bed, not thinking of packing, and trying to go to sleep again.

Very soon, Ethel came in, in a fluffy red dressing gown, her hair pushed under a thick, brown net. She adored sleeping, would go to bed early, get up late and have a two hours' siesta every afternoon, if possible. She was sad at having to get up so early this morning. And to find Maria, the cause of all this trouble, still in bed was intolerable. " I thought you would have been up a long time ago," she said.

Maria pretended she had been fast asleep, and Ethel had just woken her up. " What ? " she said, vaguely and thickly.

" I said I thought you would have been up a long time ago."

" Oh! "

" Didn't Mercedes call you at half past seven ? "

" I don't know."

" Don't be silly." Ethel felt she would like to shake her cousin.

" How was I to know ? It was very early whenever it was."

" Oh, *do* get up."

" Why ? "

Ethel gave a loud, angry sigh and came nearer the bed. Maria, who had kept her eyes closed till now, opened them and looked at her cousin. " Why was I called so early ? "

" You've got to pack before half-past eight."

" I think it was quite unnecessary, calling me so early." Maria propped herself up on one elbow and looked at Ethel. " It was an act of spite."

" Don't be silly. What about your packing ? "

" I don't need as much time to pack as you think I do."

" You need quite a lot of time."

" How much time do you think I need ? "

" Don't talk to me like that, and *do* get up."

" How was I talking to you ? How much time do you think I need ? "

" If you're going to be rude, I shall just go away."

" All right."

Mercedes' friend called for the luggage to take it on to the station in advance. He was very expensive, far more expensive than a taxi because, he said, he was running a risk.

At first, both Mercedes and Ethel were to accompany her to the station but later it was decided that it was now safe enough for her to go with Ethel alone.

Miss Pearson arrived only five minutes before Maria left the house.

" Good morning, Miss Pearson," said Maria, with an aggressive brightness. " My packing's done and I'm perfectly ready."

Miss Pearson gave her a sharp good morning and talked to Ethel. " Did that man come for the luggage ? "

" Yes," said Ethel, " he was very punctual. It must be at the station by now."

" He's a blackleg," said Maria, " the kind of person who ruins a strike. I don't like having to employ him."

" If it weren't for him you wouldn't be able to go back to England," said Miss Pearson, sternly.

" Well, I don't particularly want to go back to England at the moment. What you mean is if it weren't for him you wouldn't get rid of me so soon."

No one said anything, and Maria poured herself out another cup of coffee. Her swallowing seemed louder than she'd ever heard it, in this silence. " Anyhow, he makes a lot of money out of it. I wonder if Mercedes gets a small commission ? "

Ethel went to get ready to accompany Maria to the station, and Maria was left alone with Miss Pearson. " I'm sorry," she said, " I don't really think you want to get rid of me—or if you do it's justifiable. I'm sure it's because you want me to be in time for the beginning of term."

" You'd better get your hat and coat," said Miss Pearson, coldly.

When it came to saying goodbye, Miss Pearson did not relent, and sat firmly in front of her coffee, making it quite clear that she was not going to accompany Maria to the front door.

" Goodbye, Miss Pearson," said Maria, " and thank you very much for letting me stay here and being so kind to me."

" Goodbye, dear. Aren't you going to wear a hat ? "

" No. I don't think so."

" Very well, but you'll get filthy travelling without a hat."

" I'll get filthy anyhow, I think." She was suddenly seized with the desire to make everything up before leaving, and repeated: " Thank you very much for letting me stay here," adding, with sincerity, " and I really have enjoyed staying here. I shall miss those delicious arroces and salmonetes. I shall never forget those meals."

Miss Pearson made no response, but went on with her breakfast until Ethel came back and they were ready to leave.

" Goodbye," she said to Maria. Maria bent down and she gave her a dry peck on the cheek. " You'd better not miss your train."

" Goodbye," said Maria, and gave her a warm kiss. " Should Ethel go with me when there's a strike on ? "

" The strike's practically over now. The buses and trams will be running to-morrow."

Ethel and Maria had to walk to the station. It was some distance, a good half hour, and Ethel took very small steps. The weather was thundery and oppressive. Maria felt depressed by Miss Pearson's unrelenting attitude. She could so easily have made things all right by being nice at the end. " Miss Pearson's very glad I've gone," she said to Ethel. " She needn't have made it so clear, though."

No strikers were to be seen, and there were few guardias. Women dressed in black and carrying large baskets might have been on their way to market and others with short black lace mantillas over their heads were obviously on their way to or from Mass. It looked as though the strike was dying down without turning into a proper rising. Maria was disappointed.

At the station, Ethel began to fuss. " If you go and get your ticket," she said, " I'll go and look for the luggage."

Maria loathed Ethel trying to be practical, because she knew her cousin was really helpless and incompetent. " Perhaps it isn't there," she said, to rattle her. " Perhaps that man's stolen it. He may be one of the strikers getting his own back on people who employ blacklegs."

The booking office, though open, would not be issuing tickets for London for another ten minutes. Maria found a flustered Ethel, still looking for the luggage, and told her this. " I'll phone some one up," she said, " to fill in time."

She couldn't find a phone box in the station and had to go to a café across the road. She dialled Alonso's number and when she heard the phone ringing the other end was tempted to replace the receiver. She knew he wouldn't be up, although he had suggested she should phone. She felt rather sick after her sleepless night and hurried breakfast, and there was a buzzing in her head. A maid answered the phone.

" Is Señor Alonso there ? "

" He's not up."

" Oh."

" Who is it speaking ? "

" It doesn't matter, then."

" Who did you say you were ? "

" Oh, it doesn't matter. Please don't wake him up. I'll phone later."

There was no reply, and after saying " Hullo " twice, Maria realised that the maid must have gone to fetch him. He might be furious and she wished she'd never phoned.

" Allo," said the maid's voice.

" Hullo."

" I'm afraid the Señorito's asleep. I knocked on his door, but there was no answer."

Maria thought she was laughing at her. " It's quite all right. It doesn't matter."

" Would you like to leave a message ? "

" No thank you."

Ethel was waiting with the man and the luggage. " If you get your ticket now," she said, crossly, " this man can take the luggage to the train for us. There aren't any porters, you know."

" Is the train here ? "

" Yes, it's just come in."

When they were safely installed in the train and the man had been paid, Maria could think of nothing to say to her cousin. She smiled at her weakly to fill in the gap, and finally said, " Don't bother to wait, Ethel dear. It's so dreary waiting and you've got a long walk back."

" I'll see you off."

" I'll be all right by myself, really. . . ."

" Well, if you don't want me to see you off. . . ."

" I do. I think it's very nice of you to see me off, but I think it must be rather dull for you."

Ethel looked at her watch. " I think you've got another quarter of an hour," she said despondently.

" Well, please don't wait. Miss Pearson probably needs you for something or other."

" I'd like to be in time for Mass. Perhaps I *will* go."

" After all, I think we've remembered everything. There aren't any more messages you want me to take ? "

" No, dear. Give everyone my love."

" Goodbye, Ethel dear, and have a nice time here."

" I hope you have a nice journey." They kissed each other on both cheeks.

There were very few people travelling, probably on account of the strike, and Maria had a compartment to herself. She opened her smallest suitcase and took out a notebook. The paper was squared, as it was really one of those exercise books Spanish children use in school. She drew lines across the squares in one corner and then matched it symmetrically in the corner opposite. She turned over the page and wrote:

Dear Alonso,

I'm writing before the train leaves the station, because once it starts moving, it's very difficult to write at all legibly. I rang you up this morning and you were still asleep. I'm very glad they didn't wake you, and I hope you're still asleep (she crossed out " still asleep " because it had occurred once before and wrote " asleep now.") Thank you for being so nice to me before and during the strike.

Yours, Maria.

She read through it, saw she hadn't said a word she wanted to say, turned over the page and began again:

Darling Alonso,

I wish you had been up when I phoned, and I almost wish they had woken you up, in fact I do wish they'd woken you up. I know I was silly yesterday, and it would have been nice if the last impression you had of me had not been that. It probably does not matter much, but at the moment I can't help feeling it does. I am glad you were very fond of me, and it was silly of me to assume that you wanted that to develop or anything. You never did or said anything which could have made me think so when I come to think of it.

> Please write to me as soon as possible. I shall miss you so much. There will never be anyone who makes me. . . .

There was a jerk and she saw the platform begin to move away. She looked out of the window in case, by some chance, Alonso had decided to see her again before she went away. He would arrive just in time to see the train going off. There was no one on the platform who looked at all like him.

She closed the window to avoid smuts and sank back into her seat. She read the two letters she'd written and added to the second, in a wild scrawl caused by the motion of the train :

> The train has started, and it's impossible to write any more now, but I'll finish this when I'm waiting for my train in Paris.

She thought it would be nice to see Renteria and Pasajes again and, forgetting the smuts, let down the window and leant out. Renteria had not recovered from the floods of the previous year, and from the train one could see half ruined houses. It was neither a suburb of San Sebastian, nor altogether a small town on its own. In Pasajes harbour there were three large ships, and the sea was calm and a greyish blue.

She stopped leaning out of the window and looked at her letters once more. She tore them out of the note book and put her hand out of the window to scatter them in pieces. She watched them fly behind with such force that they would have gone into the window of the next compartment if it had been open.

She thought how extraordinary it would be if Alonso went for a walk one day and found a piece of squared paper with her handwriting on it near Pasajes.

She turned her head away from the window because the wind was blowing dust into her eyes. That made her hair blow right over her face. With a gesture of impatience she raised her hand to push it back, and burst into tears.

PART TWO

MADRID. EASTER 1936

1

IT was two years since Maria had been to Spain. Now she had won a prize which was given with the proviso that the winning student should work in a certain library at Madrid. During the past year and a half she had corresponded irregularly with Alonso, at longer and longer intervals as time went on. His letters were short and gay, and covered in drawings, portraits from memory of Maria, of himself getting fatter and fatter, of Miss Pearson and Pomti Pom. There had also been a Popeye the Sailor phase when every letter had " El Popeye " or Olive Oyl, and he hinted at some Popeye drawing concern in which he was involved.

Once or twice he met Miss Pearson and Ethel in the street, but he never called at the flat again. In one letter he wrote : " I saw Miss Pearson to-day walking down the Bulevar and I followed her at a distance for a long time because it reminded me of you. What nostalgia! "

When she wrote that she would be in Madrid for the Easter vacation, he answered saying he would make a point of being there then, and she must phone his house as soon as she arrived, no matter what time of the day it was.

She took the night train from San Sebastian to Madrid and slept until the light came leaking through the ends of the blinds. They were in the middle of the Castillian plain. The scene was unlike anything she had ever seen or imagined—and she had often had vivid pictures in her mind of what Castille must be like. The ground was flat, reddish and covered with great stones which looked like some massive litter thrown down from a height and smashed into irregular fragments. There were a few stunted twisted trees. No one seemed to live there, although faint tracks wound between the boulders. The pale morning sky, blue overhead and yellow at the horizon line, merged into the red of the earth. It was like the view, she thought, an insect might have of a pebbly yard.

The station was small for a capital. There were few people about besides the porters. It was still early, and knowing how late everything began in Spain, she decided to walk from the station into the centre of the town, first leaving her luggage in the left luggage office.

Her Spanish was rusty after so long an absence, and she kept failing to recall the simplest words when she needed them. She had never felt so much of a foreigner.

Shutters were still closed and only a few workmen in bright blue and the inevitable women in shiny black could be seen in the streets. Shops were shut, and cafés, though open, were empty. She looked into one or two, not knowing what to do with her time and wishing it was much later, but there was no one in them who looked as though they might serve her. She walked for some time, past the houses of the poor, hovels whose windows had no glass, but were just holes pierced in the walls; past richer houses whose ground floor windows were protected by bars, sometimes curved and baroque in appearance ; past the edge of a gloomy park, her legs feeling weak and strange after the journey.

It was very cold and the day had not yet become itself, but was still an after-taste of the day before. Nearer the centre of the town she was glad to see some tradespeople in the street and to hear them whistling and talking. She had heard that the people of Madrid were very friendly and that men were always paying compliments, elaborate and witty, to girls they passed in the street, but no compliments came her way, no one took the slightest notice of her. She thought everyone she met looked sad. In San Sebastian complexions had varied, but here all were sallow, black-eyed, black-haired with high cheek bones and marked nostrils.

At the bottom of a long wide street, called Eduardo Dato, she saw a taxi and called it. " Would you take me to a large café in the Gran Via," she said, because she had heard that the Gran Via was the central part of the town.

" This is the Gran Via."

" Well, I want the most central part of the Gran Via."

" All right," said the driver drily, " the Gran Via is very long."

She thought of buying a map of Madrid which she could study in a café until it was late enough to phone Alonso, but there were no shops open.

The taxi stopped outside a large, modern café, called the Negresco. Here there were no waiters, but only three old women scrubbing the floor. The chairs were standing on the tables which had been pushed together in the centre of the room. An upholstered seat ran along the wall, and Maria nervously went over to it and sat down, afraid that someone would turn her out because it was too early. Any books or notebooks which might have occupied her were left in her luggage at the station. In her handbag there were two old letters, a bill and an address book, which she looked at for some time. She powdered her face and tried to clean her nails with a match. To make the time pass, she checked it by counting sixties, but after five minutes of this she gave up. She tried to catch the eye of one of the women, and failing to do this, went over to them. Her Spanish had still deserted her and she had great difficulty in asking whether it would be possible for her to have a cup of coffee.

" Yes," said one of the women, " they'll be arriving soon."

" Do you think I could use the phone ? "

" As soon as someone comes."

The streets were still fairly empty, but the buses and trams that went by were crowded with people going to work. A few women in black wearing mantillas passed on their way to church.

A waiter appeared at the back of the café and began to arrange the counter and lay out ashtrays. Maria plucked up her courage and clapped for him. He didn't hear, and she tried again. He heard this time and looked to see where the sound came from. After doing some more to the counter and exchanging remarks with the women who were cleaning the floor, he came over to her table.

" Could I have a large white coffee ? " said Maria.

" Yes, Señorita.   You're very early."

" Am I too early ? "

" It's never too early."   He smiled kindly.

Maria wondered what this could mean.   " I'm glad you think so," she said.   " And do you think I could use your phone ? "

" In a few minutes."

He went off, putting some chairs on to the floor on his way. More waiters appeared at the back of the café.   They took no notice of Maria, although they saw her and went round arranging tables and talking to each other.   They all looked handsome in the distance, dark-skinned and shiny-haired, like foreign waiters in London, but with a more independent manner as though they had important lives of their own outside the café, which they never shed.

Maria's waiter came back with the coffee.   " Do you want to phone now ? "

" Yes, please."   She followed him to the counter.

" English ? "

" Yes."

" Do you know how to work it ? "

" No."

" Well, you put in a disc instead of coins."   He noticed her worried expression.   " Shall I get the number for you ? "

" Yes, please."   She handed him her address book where the number was written down and gave him full instructions. " And say they must wake him up—it's important."

He looked at her with understanding and was most emphatic. " Please wake him up," he insisted, to whoever was at the other end of the phone.   " It's very urgent—very."   Also he refused to leave any name and handed her the receiver triumphantly.

" Hullo," said Maria.

" Hullo."   It was Alonso.

She tried to explain who she was.   Alonso pretended not to understand.   " Maria ? " he said, " an English Maria ?   San Sebastian ?   But Maria's not an English name."

" It is if you pronounce it differently."

" How should you pronounce it ? "

" Oh, Alonso, either you know who I am or you don't."

She could hear him laughing. " Where are you ? When did you get here ? "

" Just now. I'm at the Negresco."

" That's a smart café to start on."

" It isn't at the moment. I'm the only person here."

" Poor Maria."

" Do come here soon."

" At once."

When she returned to her coffee it was cold, so she drank it up and ordered some more.

Alonso arrived soon. He walked into the café, looked round and smiled when he found her sitting in the corner. He hurried over to her, sat down beside her and kissed her hand.

" Ah, Maria, how wonderful to see you again! I can't believe it! How wonderful you look! " He rolled his eyes in mock ecstasy and made extravagant gestures, making what he said a parody of what he might have said.

He looked more melancholy than before, although he was smiling, but that may have been because Maria was not yet accustomed again to Spanish faces, and everyone looked sad to her. He was thinner and wore a dark suit as he did when he first visited Miss Pearson.

She eyed him silently. After the long wait in the café, her excitement had disappeared and she felt rather flat.

" Well," said Alonso, meeting her eye.

" You got here very quickly."

" I didn't shave."

" Perhaps that's why you look different."

" I always get older and fatter."

" I think you're thinner and not so. . . . Oh, I can't think of the Spanish for it—' smug '— "

" Smug ? "

" Oh, I've forgotten all my Spanish."

" Your accent isn't what it was." He held both her hands and went on looking at her. " I didn't really believe I'd ever see you again."

" Why ? "

C

He shrugged his shoulders, called the waiter and ordered some coffee for himself. " Well, Maria, what kind of a journey did you have ? "

" Nice. No, it wasn't really. I met a French woman, Señora del Arbol. . . ."

" That's not a French name."

" She was married to a Spaniard."

" Then she wasn't French."

" She was, by birth. . . ."

" Del Arbol." He laughed. " I've never heard such a name. You made it up."

" You can't start laughing at me so soon."

" I wasn't."

" You were. Anyhow we won't go on with it."

" We won't quarrel about it." He kissed her hand again and looked at it. " I suppose you're still as quarrelsome as ever," he smiled at her.

" I saw the Castilian plain, but I missed the Escurial. It was wonderful."

" Which ? "

" Oh, Alonso. I was so excited to be in Spain again, and then when I got here no one was up, it was so cold and there was nothing to do, and now you try and damp everything I say."

" I don't mean to."

" I never realised how much I liked Spain. As soon as I crossed the frontier and people were talking Spanish, I felt so pleased."

" And aren't you pleased to see me ? "

" Oh yes, of course. Spain is very largely you."

He encouraged her to be excited again, and in doing so became excited himself. He began to sketch out what they would do, now that she was in Madrid. " We'll start on the Prado this morning."

" I must find somewhere to stay first."

" Don't you know of anywhere ? "

" No, except where Señora del Arbol told me, and I don't want to go there."

Alonso thought for a moment. He didn't feel like being

practical. " I ought to know of a lot of Pensions," he said, " but I can't think of any." He thought again. " I'll tell you what I'll do. I'll phone Pepe. He's a student and must know all about these things."

He left her and went to the phone. The café was waking up now. All the chairs and tables were in place and two elderly men were having breakfast. A beggar was standing outside the window. He was forbidden to come inside and looked fixedly at Maria as though trying to hypnotise her to go out and give him some money. He had high cheekbones, curling nostrils and was covered with deep wrinkles. He was probably a gipsy. Maria looked the other way.

When Alonso came back to the table she noticed that there were pouches under his eyes and he looked ill. " Pepe will be here almost immediately," he said. " He lives just round the corner. Let's have a drink."

" I should be ill if I drank now."

" Let's have some more coffee, then. These glasses don't hold anything."

" Do you still drink a lot ? "

" More, I think."

" You'll get ill in the end."

" Marichu, don't try and reform me. You can't be one of those women who devote themselves to saving people. I probably won't drink so much now that you're here." He picked up her hand again. " I'll be quite different."

" Why ? "

" It was very necessary that you should come now."

" Why ? "

" I don't know." He smiled. " I wonder how you'll like Pepe. He's a socialist all right—you'll like that. Everyone is political in Madrid now."

" You're not."

" I'll have to be soon. Political or surrealist."

" Never mind."

" I don't. Are you free all today ? "

" Yes. I ought to go to the library some time. I have to work t a library you know."

" You needn't do much work. Now that you're here we *will*
have a nice time," said Alonso excitedly. " We will."

Soon a tall young man with blazing eyes and a mop of black
wavy hair came towards their table. He had a very curly face,
a cleft chin and a red mouth. He looked serious and only
smiled for a moment when he recognised Alonso. " How are
you, Alonso ? " he said, and sat down.

" Maria, this is Pepe. Pepe, this is an English girl who wants
to find a nice Pension."

" How do you do ? " said Pepe, and shook hands with her so
violently that she winced. Afeer that he fixed his eyes on the
table and said nothing.

" Would you like some coffee ? " said Alonso.

Pepe shook his head.

" And how are things going with you ? " said Alonso.

" All right."

" A lot of party work, as usual ? "

" Yes. Did you see that demonstration on Sunday ? "

" Only for a moment."

" What did you think of it ? Pretty banners, weren't they ? "

" Yes, but I think it was a bad idea."

" It wasn't. It was a splendid example of unity. Do you
realise that every party of the Left was represented ? Even the
anarchists came in with us."

" I still think it was a mistake." Alonso enjoyed baiting him.

" A mistake ! " Pepe curled his lip and then leant forward
and banged the table with his fist. " We've got to do all we can.
We've got to demonstrate the whole time, otherwise nothing
will get done. Did you hear what happened in the Castellana
the other night ? "

" Yes."

" Well, that's the kind of thing we're up against—and then
you say it's a mistake."

" What happened in the Castellana ? " asked Maria.

Pepe showed no inclination to tell her, so Alonso did. " A
band of fascists shot some communists."

" They shot eleven unarmed workers," said Pepe. He shook
his head, genuinely distressed.

" That's why I think these demonstrations a mistake," said Alonso, calmly. " They simply provoke the reactionaries."

" It isn't the demonstrations that provoke them," Pepe laughed, angrily, and fixed his burning eyes on Alonso. " It's the fact that they've got all the arms and the money—and we haven't—and they'll go on having them unless we do something about it."

" But how can they have all the arms if it's a Popular Front Government ? " asked Maria.

" They've got eighty per cent. of the army." Pepe threw back the lock which kept falling into his eyes. " The Government knows that and it doesn't clean up the army. If some officer goes round doing fascist propaganda nothing happens to him, he's just sent to the provinces. It's the same with the Guardia Civil. There are very few of their leaders you can trust. And the Government doesn't do anything. It doesn't dare. That's why *we've* got to demonstrate. We mustn't all be intimidated! "

" I see," said Maria.

Alonso leant over to her and whispered in her ear, " He's only seventeen."

Pepe took no notice of this whispering. " What's the use of having the majority of the people, the large majority for you ? " he went on and banged the table again, " if the people against you have control of the arms and money ? " He buried his face in his hands. " It's terrible, that Castellana business—terrible."

Alonso waited tactfully a few minutes before he reminded him of other things. " What about a Pension ? "

" All the ones I know are full," said Pepe and leapt up. " I must be going. I've got a lot to do." He shook hands with them and rushed away.

" I wonder why he thought I'd asked him here," said Alonso. " He can't have imagined I wanted to discuss a demonstration." He turned to Maria, who was looking very gloomy after hearing about the Castellana business. " He's furious with me," he laughed. " He can't bear anyone to criticise the party at all. Still," he smiled indulgently, " he's very young."

" He's probably right. Is it really true about those workers ? "

" As true as anything is if you haven't actually seen it."

" Then he's probably right. I think it's awful."

" Not as awful as it will be if there are more like him about."
He caught Maria's eye and smiled. " Well, Marichu, darling,
that hasn't got us very far. We'll never find you a Pension at
this rate, will we ? " He called the waiter and paid the bill,
although Maria protested and told him she was quite rich now,
because she'd won a prize. He laughed at her prize and her
academic future. " If you go on like that," he said, " you'll end
up a wizened little thing one only sees behind a desk. I see now
that I must try and stop you working as much as I can."

As they walked down the Calle de Alcala, he pointed out
everything which was typically Madrileño. A great many very
modern looking cafés had sprung up in Madrid recently, which
had no relation at all to the architecture around them. Alonso
delighted in their vulgarity and their insides of chromium and
shiny red or black. " Before we know where we are it will be
like New York," he said. He spoke as though he loved Madrid.
" You can't criticise anything about Madrid. It's not pretty
and it's not well planned, but it's nice."

He smiled at her and pressed his fingers into her elbow. She
noticed how the narrowness of his finely moulded mouth made
his smile taut and cruel. His face was more emphasised than the
face she had known in San Sebastian, like a painting carried
one stage further. The skin was looser and hung more on the
moulding.

He hurried her to the Prado, and when they arrived, rushed
her through the rooms, laughing at everything she said. " You
don't know anything at all about painting," he said, " even if
you are too learned in other ways."

At last they came to a room where there was no one else. He
stopped facing her, made her turn towards him and held both
her hands. He looked straight at her for a long time. He moved
his head closer to her's very slowly until they could see nothing
but each other's eyes. " Now shut one eye," he said, and she
saw only a huge black pupil full of floating lights.

" It makes me feel like St. John of the Cross," he said,
laughed and released her. " Now we'll leave the Prado and find
you a home."

2

" I'd like to have a room looking on to the Gran Via, a central part of the Gran Via," said Maria, so they tried Pensions in Alcala and Pi y Margal. They looked out for the sign, and when they were high enough up (because Pensions on the ground floor or first floor were usually more expensive) went in and asked for a room. It was very difficult to find one. The same thing happened every time, the proprietor or his wife would start a conversation, asked Maria how long she wanted to stay, what kind of a room she would like, as though there were plenty of rooms to be had, and then at a given moment they would announce unexpectedly that they were full up and murmur something about the number of tourists in Spring. After this had happened five times, they were tired and disheartened, and Alonso decided something was very wrong.

" I think they think you're my little friend," he said, " and we want a room for immoral purposes."

" Yes, that must be it."

" Well, you'd better try the next place by yourself, and I'll wait in a café."

" I didn't realise Spanish Pensions were so respectable."

" They're not, if you go the right way about it, but this must be the wrong way—that's if we were going about it at all."

The next sign they saw was at the top of Eduardo Dato, only just central enough for Maria, and this time she went in alone. She had no difficulty at all, but her heart sank when the proprietress called her husband and her son to discuss it. However, she had only done this because they were both proud of their English and did not often have an opportunity of showing it off. The three of them showed Maria into a large room with two cupboards, running water and a table with drawers where she could work. There were two French windows with small, iron balconies outside from which she could see the corner where Eduard Dato joined Pi y Margal, while directly opposite her loomed a huge, modern cinema where Charlie Chaplin was showing in " Modern Times."

They were all very pleased when Maria complimented them

on their English which was poor. The son offered to go to the station for her luggage and Maria handed over her ticket.

When she joined Alonso he was relieved to find her settled. If they had had to go on looking for a room much longer, he said, they would have burst into tears.

They lunched at a German restaurant because he couldn't think of anywhere else to go, and ate large helpings of Vienna schnitzels and sauté potatoes. They were given a room to themselves and sat at a large table meant for at least eight people and used by tertulias : evening gatherings of a regular circle centering round a leading spirit, who might be a writer or other personality.

After lunch, they walked to a café. The streets were deserted and the shops were shut. " Everybody goes home in the middle of the day," said Alonso.

" Like San Sebastian."

" All over Spain."

He took her to La Granja, one of the less modern looking cafés in the Gran Via, where she might, if she was lucky, he said, see a famous Spanish writer or painter. The place was pretty empty. He pointed to a fat, bearded man, sitting alone in a corner. " That man is a fairly well-known architect." He looked around. " And down there is a painter whom no one's ever heard of. That's the best I can do for you."

It was a large room, with a patio at the end farthest from the street. A gallery ran round the patio. The walls were tiled and some of the tiles had drawings on them which, at a distance, looked as though they had been done there by artistic customers, but were, in fact, printed by a machine.

After coffee, they walked round the Puerto del Sol. He showed her a café which bullfighters frequented. He seemed restless and kept suggesting things they might do. " You mustn't be bored for a minute," he kept repeating.

They ended up on a bench in the Retiro. There were no flowers out and the trees were bare. Some small children played beneath the trees while their nurses or governesses sat and watched them.

" That's what I used to have to do," said Maria.

" Poor thing."

She felt tired and shivered slightly.

" Do you find it cold ? "

" Yes, very. I thought it was going to be warm here."

" It's the Gulf Stream. It's upsetting everything."

They watched a race between three little boys and then walked to the pond. Alonso dropped stones into the water and listened to the sound they made. " The smaller ones have a higher note than the others," he said.

When his pile of stones was finished, Maria collected more from the gravel and gave them to him. He was touched by this and kissed her hand. After that he stood with his arm round her while they both watched the stones going in.

3

After the Retiro, Maria felt so tired that Alonso insisted that she should get a few hours' sleep before doing any more. They took the metro to the Pension. The Madrid metro was small and rickety looking. There was only one way in and one way out, and it was easy to find one's way about. The train itself was pretty, a light colour, square and fragile. There were only three small carriages.

She slept until seven and then lay in bed, still exhausted, looking out of the window. The noises of the traffic were unfamiliar, the motor horns louder and more aggressive than in England, the rattle of the trams more metallic. It was dark and the moving illuminations from the cinema across the road flashed into the room at regular intervals lighting up the cupboard.

She lay dazed until Alonso rang her up and still in a dream dressed slowly to go out to dinner. They went to a smart, expensive Italian restaurant, of which Alonso was particularly fond. He looked round the room excitedly and then led her to a table by the wall. " I'll sit next to you and then we can both see her. I love that lady."

The lady he referred to was sitting at the table immediately in front of them facing them. She was very old, shrivelled, wrinkled and heavily made up. Her features were distinguished, her nose thin and hooked, her chin firm. Her sunken cheeks were a paler shade of her lipstick, her heavy lids were a purplish blue, her white hair had a pale mauve shine on it and was curled high like a wig. On the top of it, tilted forward, she wore a small black velvet hat, decorated by one sweeping ostrich feather which curled over the brim on to her shoulder. She was dressed entirely in black and wore no ornament besides the heavy rings which covered her hands. Her nails were dark red. There was something dashing in the simple lines of her clothes, something alarming in the way in which she obviously avoided anything which might soften her appearance. She wore clothes she might have worn at thirty and she must have been getting on for seventy. She bent over her plate eating slowly and greedily, never looking up.

" One of the last survivors," said Alonso. He spoke quietly so that she shouldn't hear. Maria watched her attentively.

" She's the only survivor," he went on. " All her lot must have died off by now. I've often seen her here and she's always alone. She orders her food very carefully and has long discussions about it with the head waiter." He couldn't take his eyes off her. " I think she knows I watch her. I once saw her at an exhibition, and I think there was a look of recognition in her face."

" How thin she must be," said Maria.

" Aren't you glad you've seen her ? "

" Yes."

" I'm glad you've seen her. I do like people with style."

" Oh."

He knew what she was thinking and smiled at her. " You haven't any."

" I don't want any."

Alonso ordered dinner with more care than usual and talked

to the waiter for a long time. " How I wish I'd lived seventy years ago," he said.

" I don't."

" Do you know what her name is ? She's of French origin, and I don't know why she's ended up in Madrid."

" I think she looks very cruel."

The head waiter had gone over to the table in front of them and was talking animatedly to the old lady. Now that she was no longer looking down at her food, one could see her bright, black eyes and her thin, drooping mouth. They listened and heard her discuss the various tascas in the low parts of Madrid. As she talked, her mouth trembled and she folded and unfolded her hands. She insisted that the sherry in the place she knew was better than anywhere else. The head waiter disagreed with her. She suggested that they should go together and find out when he had an evening off. He agreed delightedly. He was also old, though not as old as she was.

Alonso was enthralled. " What a marvellous creature she is ! How superbly she handles her relation with him ! What real *joie de vivre*."

" I think perhaps you're a snob."

Alonso kissed her hand and laughed. " Marichu, darling. How I like your point of view. You see things so clearly. She looks cruel and I'm a snob."

" And as for *joie de vivre* . . ."

" I know what you're going to say," Alonso beamed at her. "You needn't go on with it, though it's always nice to hear you."

" You *must* treat me as an equal."

Alonso grabbed her hand excitedly and banged it down on to the seat. " This is a wonderful moment for me. In front of me is a whole world surviving by a thread, and beside me the call to arms to snip that thread. The revolution ! " He kissed her cheek. " Tell me, doesn't it cross your mind that in order for her to be able to prolong her *joie de vivre*, her style, those things are being suppressed in thousands of people ? "

" Yes it does. Not only those things . . ."

" I can't understand why you don't get on better with Pepe."

" Now I know you're not treating me as an equal. I know

what you think of Pepe."

The waiter arrived with some very delicious food and ceremoniously served it. Behind him came another waiter with a large bottle of red wine. Alonso turned to Maria with satisfaction and smiled.

It was impossible to resist the warm, rich smell, and after the first few mouthfuls she melted. " All the same," she said, " I don't think you really like me."

" It's quite the other way about." He drank some wine and looked at her warmly, and pointed to her glass, urging her to drink. " I love you."

" Well, we haven't anything in common."

" Never mind."

4

The library where Maria had to work was situated in the rich, residential part of Madrid, near the Castellana. Besides being a library, it was a museum. The building and everything in it had been left to an Institute for Research by the founder, a well-known scholar and collector.

Letters of recommendation had preceded her from England and everything was prepared for her arrival. She was received with great ceremony. The door was opened by a small, round man whom she discovered later to be the caretaker. She tried to explain who she was. " Ah, the English scholar! " he said, shook hands with her and hurried off to find the librarian. The librarian, Padre Moreno, came briskly down the wide marble staircase, shook hands with her, introduced himself and led her off to present her formally to two of the Trustees. The Trustees were imposing, both white haired and massive, and they shook hands with her, bowing slightly as they did so, hoped she would find everything she required, and urged her to come to them without the slightest hesitation if ever she needed anything else. As it happened, she never saw them again.

The ground floor belonged to the Trustees. The library and the museum took up all the first floor (it was a very wide house) and the rest of the house was still as it had been when the founder lived there and was kept as a kind of museum of his books, pictures, furniture and photographs.

Maria's desk was in the right wing of the library—there were only two desks there—facing the desk of Padre Moreno. It was a valuable, antique, handsome piece of furniture and had been equipped with everything she could want, pencils, rubbers, pens, blotting paper in three colours, a ruler, a paper knife, note books, loose paper and beautiful notepaper and envelopes bearing the coat of arms of the founder. Everyone from the Trustees and Padre to the caretaker and his wife declared to her that they were at her disposal.

Padre Moreno, short, dark, thin, with a sly expression, was the embodiment of Maria's idea of the Spanish Jesuit, the ultramontane, and she imagined that when he was not in the library he was in the house of some aristocrat plotting for the restoration of the Monarchy. Actually he was not a Jesuit but a secular priest, and his whole time was devoted to the library and research. He also gave Catechism lessons to some children three times a week in the library.

He was friendly, and at once showed Maria round the library and the museum. The books he liked very much and explained the workings of the catalogue with a restrained but passionate pride. His attitude to the museum was cynical, and as he flitted lightly from one priceless ceramic to another he kept saying, " It's a good specimen if you like that kind of thing." And when he came to a small broken vase he giggled, as he said, " And that's worth thousands of pesetas." After he had shown her round the main room, he looked at her slyly and laughed. " I think there are some Flemish door knockers somewhere if you'd like to see them."

Maria said it would do some other time. Finally, he was almost gallant, and when, on her third day there he showed her around the part of the house where the founder had lived, he pointed to the prettiest of the founder's daughters in a large oil-painting of the family and said, " I think you resemble her a little."

Maria mentioned this to Alonso proudly and he was delighted, but insisted that it was simply because both she and the founder's daughter had fair hair, and this, to an unworldly priest living in a country where nearly everyone was dark, must make them seem exactly alike.

He was more delighted when she told him that Padre Moreno had referred to the corruption of the church in the Middle Ages. " That," he said, " is a definite proposal."

When the next day she told him that they had abandoned the Middle Ages and were now at the counter-reformation, Alonso shook his head sadly and told her that the librarian must have changed his mind about her. He planned to write a short story round the delicate relationship of a librarian priest and a young female scholar which would consist of a series of conversations about the history of the church.

Padre Moreno, though devoted to his work, was always ready to talk. Often when Maria looked up from her book she would meet his sly glance, and after the preliminary of asking her how she was getting on and if she needed anything, he would start talking about Spanish literature and history. He had a quiet, nasal voice. His small, black eyes would dart about behind his steel-rimmed glasses, while he spoke, and he would join his hands together in front of him as though he was praying. He had a pleasant way of saying, " We scholars," which made Maria feel learned and hard-working.

The assumption that he must have a high opinion of her scholarship made her feel that she must go to the library for a long time every day and at least pretend to work. She spent two hours there in the morning and two or three hours in the after-noon. She felt a little persecuted by him, and sometimes when she was in the street with Alonso and he was pulling her ear, putting his arm round her or behaving demonstratively, she would imagine she could see the little priest on the other side of the pavement and felt very ashamed of her unscholarly behaviour. If ever she saw a small priest near them, she would

behave with great propriety for at least ten minutes, because
even if he wasn't Padre Moreno, he might be a friend of his
who knew what she looked like.

Alonso surprised her by phoning her up at nine o'clock for
several days after her arrival to say he was waiting for her in
the café beside the cinema in front of her Pension. One morning
he managed to persuade her not to go to the library, and spent
the time with her in gramophone shops teaching her to enjoy
canto jondo, the traditional guitar singing from the South, with
its Moorish affinities, and often extempore. She lunched with
him, too, but insisted on going to the library very soon after
lunch despite his protest.

When she saw Padre Moreno, she lied to him and said she
had not felt well in the morning. Although she looked the
picture of health, he believed her and was worried. " Is it the
change of climate ? " he asked.

" Yes, I find it very cold. It's not often as cold as this in the
Spring in England."

" This is the coldest Spring for a long time."

" Perhaps it's the Gulf Stream," She wanted to find out if
anyone else knew anything about it.

" Who knows ? " sighed Padre Moreno.

The next day Alonso was again waiting at the café at nine
o'clock.

" I'd never imagined you could get up so early twice running,"
said Maria.

" Neither had I."

He had planned a delightful morning. It was sunny, though
still very cold. They could either buy some fried calamares and
eat them in the Retiro and pay a visit to the Zoo, or if that was
too cold for her they could pay another visit to the Prado and
go and see the porcelain room in the palace.

" I can't, I must go to the library," said Maria.

" Oh no, you can go there this afternoon."

" It's easier to work in the mornings."

" But you're only here for six weeks—less than that. I shall
hardly see anything of you."

" It's nice of you to want to see me, but . . ."

Alonso laughed. "It isn't because I want to see you, it's because I hate people I know working. I like my friends to be lazy like I am."

Alonso pretended to accept Maria's four hours' work a day, but he never liked it. He continued to get up in time to meet her at nine every morning and kept her away from the library until eleven. Often she lunched with him and she always met him for a drink before lunch at about a quarter to two. She lunched between two and half-past. After the library in the afternoon she would meet him again for a drink and usually had dinner with him.

Besides La Granja, he frequented a place called Baviera, where one could get very good lager beer accompanied by generous tapas (something to eat given free with the drink) of prawns, olives stuffed with pimentos, curled anchovies, crayfish. Most of the Germans in Madrid came here on account of the beer and in the evening one saw a great many large, blonde, teutonic couples sitting stolidly in front of their pints. They fascinated Alonso and his pockets were full of quick sketches of them. Maria disliked them. "You shouldn't draw them. They're so ugly," she said. "I only like Latins."

"They're satisfying to draw, like pigs." He preferred the men, and after doing the rolls of fat below the bullet-shaped skull would allow Maria to put in the bristles.

Three of Alonso's friends also frequented Baviera, Rafael, a young man with a fresh complexion, blue eyes and light brown hair, Antonio, grey faced and gloomily animated, and Jaime, who was nondescript to look at and never said anything.

Alonso didn't want to introduce Maria to anyone for the moment and looked annoyed when these three came and sat at their table one evening. Up till then he had been careful to nod to them distantly when he was with her. Rafael who was always cheerful, brought the other two along with him to tease Alonso. "So this is why we haven't seen anything of you for days," he said.

Alonso shrugged his shoulders.

"Can we sit down ?"

"Oh yes."

" I'd better introduce myself," said Rafael to Maria as he saw Alonso wouldn't do it. He presented the other two and they all shook hands with her in turn.

Rafael fixed his light, smiling eyes on her face and asked her how she liked Madrid, what nationality she was and what she thought of Spaniards. " Don't judge us all by Alonso here! " He hardly waited for her answers, but chatted on, telling her what she ought to see during her stay. He paid for a round of beer, much to Alonso's annoyance.

On hearing that she was studying Spanish literature, the gloomy faced Antonio became interested, and talked for a long time about the reign of Philip IV and how it was necessary to have a rich aristocracy who could patronise the arts.

As they left, Rafael said they must have another meeting, and Antonio added, " We must have another interesting talk." He had done all the talking and she had not been able to get a word in edgeways. Jaime merely shook hands and bowed slightly.

All this irritated Alonso. " Now every time we come to Baviera, they'll be there," he said. " Rafael always smiling with his soft Galician eyes and Antonio always holding forth about the Spanish tradition. He's a terrific monarchist."

He couldn't afford to take her out to dinner that day as his money was running out, and he hated the idea of letting her pay for herself.

" It's your conventional streak," said Maria.

" It isn't a streak. I'm *completely* conventional," he said.

She dined at her Pension after which he called for her and took her to a tasca near the Puerta del Sol, where a beautiful dry sherry could be had at a very reasonable price. It was an attractive place, the walls tiled in royal blue and sea green and the floor mosaic. Tables were placed in small compartments separated by wooden partitions. Each of these compartments could have held a moderate sized tertulia, and many of them did—the muffled sound of talking and laughing never stopped. All the voices were male, but Maria was now used to being the only girl in these places, and as she was English, no one thought anything of it. They found a table to themselves.

" While you're here," said Alonso, " I should like to keep

you entirely to myself. I grudge the time you spend at the library. If only I had more money, at least you could have all your meals with me. I shall borrow."

" Oh please don't do that," said Maria, " I'm sure you're in debt as it is."

" What does it matter ? In a few weeks you'll be gone. What'll I have to spend money on then ? I can work and pay it back."

Through the partition came the clear, hard sound of plucked guitar strings, the same five-note phrase repeated again and again, always louder and ending abruptly on a downward run. A man began to sing in a high falsetto.

" Am I so important to you as all that ? " asked Maria.

" Doesn't it look like it ? You're the only person I care about at all."

" Do you love me ? "

" Of course I do."

" Why didn't you say so before ? "

" Because."

" Because what ? "

" Because you would misunderstand it."

She was baffled. He shrugged his shoulders. " If I were an Englishman I should want to marry you. If I were a Frenchman I should want an affair with you, but being the kind of Spaniard I am, I can't do either." He saw her look annoyed. " And yet, Maria, I do love you."

" And supposing I were to fall in love with you ? " she asked. " Where would I be then ? "

" You won't."

" Supposing I have already."

He laughed. " If you do it's only out of pique."

" How do you know ? "

" I think I know you very well."

He went on after a pause, " If you married me you would be wretched, and the idea of a casual affair with you is impossible for me—you know how it is with Spaniards of my class, we marry for family reasons—I shall never marry at all—and we have prostitutes. I told you I was completely conventional."

Drink and the fierce melancholy of the song had made Maria gloomy. " Oh well, I suppose it's a sort of romantic friendship," she said bitterly.

" No, it's not that either," he insisted. " Don't be angry because I try to be honest with you. Believe it or not, you are the only thing that matters in my life."

5

Maria awoke the next morning with a headache. Like Alonso, she, too, had her convention in these matters. Young men came and went in her life rather frequently, and she regarded it as a duty to sleep with them. Her feelings about Alonso were in a dimension which seemed different to those she had previously experienced, but she took it for granted that her behaviour ought to follow the pattern to which she was accustomed. She did not believe that his convention could be more than an excuse on his part. Perhaps it was an affectation, a wish to be different, a wish to keep her guessing.

Alonso did not meet her before the library that morning, for as he explained later, he, too, had a headache. When she did meet him in the evening he was still preoccupied with procuring money from somewhere in order to be able to take her out.

" If only I had the Popeye contract now! " he said. He explained what it was. In the summer of 1935, drinking whisky by himself at the shiny bar of the Bar Basque, he had been approached by a tall, red-faced man who was also on his own and wanted to talk to someone. This man had asked him what he thought of the decorations on the walls, and to get rid of him Alonso said he thought they were frightful, and it was no use expecting him to think anything of such things, because he was a great artist, perhaps the greatest artist in Spain.

" You're just the man I want," said the man. " I'm a publisher, and I've just secured the copyright for Popeye children's books. There's a lot of money in it."

Alonso took a proud line and asked how this could possibly concern him. The man begged him to consider it, and bought him a great many double whiskies, repeating again and again, " There'd be a lot of money in it for you."

At last, Alonso asked how much.

" Six hundred pesetas a month."

Alonso laughed with scorn.

" Six hundred pesetas a week, I mean," said the man.

In the end they agreed on eight hundred pesetas a week, which at that time was worth a little under twenty pounds. The job was to last three months, at so many drawings per week.

The next morning, unsure whether the incident had been real or a dream, Alonso found the publisher's card in his pocket and hurried off to his office to make sure of his twenty pounds a week contract. To his surprise he was received rather coldly. There would be plenty of others willing to take it on, the man said, he had offered it to the first comer, because time was all important. However, one needn't be the best artist in Spain to do a thing like that, and eight hundred was out of the question. Alonso could take it or leave it at six hundred (rather less than fifteen pounds), but he must decide at once. Alonso took it.

He organised his family into what he described as a small capitalist system of his own. His sisters and cousins worked under him. He sketched the outline and they inked in the lines and filled in the black parts, drew a square round it and wrote in the words inside the balloon. He paid them the lowest possible wages and was left with a large profit.

After three months of it, he gambled away most of the money in Biarritz and St. Jean de Luz. Every time he put pencil to paper, a Popeye appeared and he felt very tired. " Still, it was worth it," he said. " I love gambling. But I wish I'd kept some till now. If only I'd known you were coming! "

" But you knew I might, I said so."

" I didn't think you meant it."

The following days she saw little of Alonso by himself. In

Baviera they were joined by Rafael and his friends, in La Granja by some others. Alonso was still thinking about money, outlining to her what wonderful things they could do, trips to all the principal towns of Castille, meals at the most expensive restaurants every day, and presents for her of books, canto jondo records, and anything else she fancied.

"But I'm perfectly happy as I am," she said, "anyone would think I was a gold digger or something. For goodness sake forget about money, and if you want to see more of me, then let me pay for myself."

6

One evening, coming back from the library, Maria found an enormous crowd in Calle Alcala. People overflowed from the pavements on to the road so that the traffic could only advance at a snail's pace. Drivers shouted at pedestrians to clear the way, but no one took the slightest notice of them. The noise was deafening, motor hooters, shouting and a kind of distant roar.

Maria's tram was held up. She looked out and saw about six stationary trams ahead and more behind. Several passengers decided to get out and walk. Others began to talk to each other excitedly. The conductor questioned a man in the street.

"What is it?" Maria asked.

"More trouble. There's been shooting."

Finally, she decided to get out and walk, too. It was impossible to get to the further, less crowded pavement, because the traffic would take any opportunity to advance, jerking forward suddenly with no regard to anyone in front, a maddened stream of car drivers, taxi drivers, tram drivers, so she was forced to the nearer pavement, there to be swallowed up by the crowd, all moving downward and bearing her along with them.

Struggling to keep upright, she edged her way to the side where she might find a doorway in which to shelter until the crowd had passed on, but they were all full already, and she was forced to go further and further in the wrong direction.

Several times she asked, " What is it ? " but was either given no answer or told that no one knew yet. Most of the crowd, like herself, seemed to have been caught up in this by accident. At the bottom of the long street where it turned out into a sort of open square, she could see some Guardia Civil, some mounted, watching the crowd without moving.

People at the back began to run, pushing the others forward. A panic was beginning. Distant shots were heard. She hurried on with the others, terrified because she was small and entirely hedged in so that she had no idea of what was happening or where she was going.

Everyone began to run. There were more shots. Now her heart was beating so hard that she could hardly breathe. She decided to act at once, before she was trampled on, and summoning every ounce of strength she possessed, fought her way to the side, pushing ruthlessly with her elbows. There was no doorway for her, but she flattened herself against the wall, standing on her toes so that they should not project far and would have less chance of being trodden on. She stayed there firmly, although many tried to push her on, her arms and legs getting knocked, and at one moment an umbrella pressed so hard against her thigh that she thought it would go through her, and almost broke it as she pushed it away.

At last, after a long time, the crowd thinned a little and she could move along the wall, taking care to keep close to it all the time. Those in front of her turned off to the right down the first side street and started to run. She did the same, but sticking to the wall the whole time. The people round her halted abruptly, faced by a number of others rushing down on them from the other end of the street. She saw a doorway, ran to it and stayed there.

The door was open and led into a corridor. Here a number were taking refuge. A young couple, several old men and some women stood in a group and talked very fast.

" It was much worse there," said a man.

" Oh, not nearly so bad," said another.

" Much worse," said the first, " there were no guardias."

" Where was it much worse ? " Maria asked the young couple, as they were the nearest to her. She thought she spoke plainly, but perhaps something peculiar had happened to her Spanish.

" Alcala," they said.

" Worse than where ? " she persisted.

" Alcala."

She couldn't make out what they meant and wondered if she had been talking English. " If it's Alcala they're talking about . . ." she said.

" Yes, Alcala," the girl interrupted, smiling at her indulgently as though she were a child or a half-wit.

" Well, if it was Alcala," said Maria, quite angry by now, " there *are* guardias there. I've just come from there and I saw them."

" Yes, there are guardias," said the girl, with the same indulgent smile, and Maria gave up. She stayed at the edge of the group and tried to hear what they were saying. A lot of people were talking at once. There seemed to be an argument going on.

" No, it wasn't really burnt," said a man.

" It was burnt to the ground," said another at the same time.

" No, only some of the inside got burnt, the woodwork. You can't burn down buildings like that."

" I was talking to someone who'd seen it and they said there wasn't a stone left."

An old lady shook her head and sighed, " Jesus! Mary! I don't know what's going to happen."

Maria looked out of the door. The crowd had gone, although there were a number of people in the street standing in groups and talking. A few shots could be heard, but they sounded far away.

She asked the couple how she could get to Eduardo Dato without having to go to Alcala or Pi y Margal, and they told her.

" Are you a foreigner ? " asked the girl.

" Yes."

The girl looked at her young man, relieved. They had obviously been wondering what was the matter with her. Maria couldn't make out why they should think there was something wrong about her, and felt uncomfortable.

She had no difficulty in reaching the Pension. When she arrived, she found the proprietress, her family and the servants in the passage talking excitedly.

" I had quite a lot of difficulty in getting here," said Maria.

" What happened ? "

" I got caught in the crowd."

" Was there any shooting ? "

" A lot."

" There, what did I tell you ? " said the proprietress, turning to her son.

" Something's been burnt," said Maria.

" It's that church," said the son, " they tried to set fire to it early this afternoon.

" Who did ? " asked Maria.

" Who do you expect ? The Communists, I suppose."

" Why should they ? "

No one answered, and Maria went to her room and looked out of the window. Nothing was happening in Eduardo Dato. There was a group of mounted guardias at the corner looking down Pi y Margal.

After half an hour she phoned Alonso. He was not at home. She phoned La Granja and he was not there either. She heard nothing of him until she was half way through dinner.

He knew no more than she did. He had gone out and had turned back when there was firing. He had gone to a café near his home and then on to La Granja, hoping she would be there.

" Well, shall we meet to-morrow ? " said Maria.

" I'll get up early and see you before the library. It's the safest time."

7

The next morning, Alonso was waiting for her in the café by the cinema. He was tired, unshaven and depressed. "This kind of thing upsets one's day completely," he said.

"Yes," said Maria, "but it does excite me a little, I must confess, at least it would if I knew what was happening."

"I'm not made for revolutionary times."

They read all the papers there were in the café. There was an account of the burning of a church near the Puerta del Sol. Only the roof and some of the inside were damaged. There had been riots near the Puente de Toledo.

"What do they mean by riots?" said Maria.

"I don't know."

"Why did the Guardia Civil fire on the crowd? They weren't doing anything. They were like me."

"They were probably trying to move them along. They only fired in the air. No one was hurt."

"It says eleven people injured."

"Well, they weren't shot, I don't suppose, they were trampled on."

"Yes, but the firing caused the panic."

"Don't ask me anything about it. I don't know anything besides what the newspapers tell me."

"Why are all newpapers in cafés Right Wing?"

"I don't know that either."

When they had drunk their coffee they went to see the church. It was Maria's idea, and Alonso was not very anxious to go. There were several guardias on duty outside the church, telling a small, silent, curious crowd to keep moving. There were no signs of damage beyond a heap of wood outside the door. No one was allowed inside. Maria looked at the church carefully, then disappointed suggested they should go to a café. Alonso still gloomy, said he didn't mind what he did.

"They were very excited in the Pension," said Maria, "I think they're Fascists."

"Why?"

"Because they said the Communists must have done it."

"You think everyone's a Fascist if they don't go about like Pepe."

"I don't think Rafael's a Fascist—or you."

"You're not so sure of me."

"Yes I am."

"I can't think why. After all, I think the Communists probably did it."

"Why should they have done it any more than anyone else? I think the Fascists did it so that they could pretend the Communists did it. It's just the kind of thing they'd do."

Alonso laughed. "For goodness sake, Maria, we don't know anything about it so don't let's speculate."

They went into a small café and ordered more coffee. "You can almost tell when there's going to be trouble," said Maria, "you feel it in your bones. On the way to the library I felt something, but I didn't know what it was. Next time I shall."

"The air becomes electric. I can tell."

Alonso was silent and moody. He didn't look at her once. "I won't go to the library if you like," said Maria.

"Good." He didn't seem very pleased.

"I don't seem to have seen you properly for so long."

"You saw me the day before yesterday."

"What's the matter with you?"

"You must allow me to be myself."

"Oh, I do." She put out her hand and touched his. He smiled at her. They held hands silently for a long time, then paid the bill and left the café.

Alonso was now desperate about money. He had none left, and had been borrowing from his sisters. Now he was reduced to coaxing the cook to give him twenty-five pesetas out of the housekeeping money. As he couldn't pay her back, she would have to tell his father and there might be a fuss.

"In future I must pay," said Maria. "At least my money's my own."

"No, you can't."

After a brisk walk in the Retiro against a cold wind, they went to Baviera and drank some beer. Maria insisted on paying for it. They did not stay there long but hurried over to La Granja to drink something stronger. Alonso was in need of it.

" I must go to San Sebastian and finish a portrait," he said, " then I shall have a lot of money."

" Don't go while I'm here. It would be such a waste."

" All right, but I can't borrow money from anyone any more. If I could borrow I'd wait until you'd gone and then do the portrait and pay it back." He ordered a pernod for himself and a sherry for her.

" I didn't think you'd let your debts worry you."

" I don't mind about my debts. I want to get hold of some money."

They thought of various impracticable schemes for getting some money which only depressed Alonso more.

When it was lunch time, they both felt so miserable that they did not want to part, and Alonso allowed Maria to pay for his lunch. They found a very cheap restaurant near the Puerta del Sol, where a large carafe of red wine was thrown in with the meal. They drank half of the wine straight off.

" *I* could lend you some money," said Maria. She pulled a pencil and paper out of her bag. " I'll work out how much."

" I don't want to borrow any money off you."

" Why not ? "

" I don't." He was firm, and she put the pencil and paper away again.

After lunch, she declared she must go to the library.

" Please don't," he said. " Come for a walk with me. If I go to San Sebastian you'll be able to work undisturbed from morning till night."

" You expect *me* to give you all my time and yet you can calmly propose going off for a week or more when I've only got such a short time left here. I missed the library this morning and I must make up for it this afternoon."

She found Padre Moreno in the entrance hall of the library. He had arrived in a long, black mackintosh, below which appeared not the soutane, but trousers.

He shook hands with her and smiled, pointing to his clothes. " It's not always safe to wear one's soutane."

When he took off his mackintosh, she saw that he was wearing an ordinary collar and a spotted bow tie. He looked like a bank clerk and no longer at all sinister. "A great many of our community found it difficult to tie these things," he laughed. "But when people start burning churches!" He sighed and threw up his small, white hands.

8

Maria longed to know what was happening, or what was going to happen, and asked everyone she met what they thought. Pepe hinted, with relish, that trouble was brewing, and Rafael said he was extremely worried about the situation, but looked as cheerful as ever, but no one could really enlighten her. Everything was always put down to Communists burning churches, except by Pepe, who said it was the Anarchists, and anyhow that wasn't the point at all. Why the church was burnt and how it all started remained a mystery. Alonso was un-interested.

The only times she was alone with him were when he escorted her home from cafés or called for her to take her to one. Once she came across him by accident. She was sitting in a tram on her way to the library, looking straight ahead of her, preoccupied still with the political situation, when a low, gruff voice beside her said, "Señorita. Allow me the honour of paying for your ticket."

She was surprised and undecided whether to look at the speaker or not. This sort of thing was always flattering, especially since, during this period of unrest in Madrid, men no longer paid compliments to every passably good looking girl they met. She decided to take no notice.

"Ah, please Señorita, allow me this honour." The voice was ridiculously gruff and low. It was also rather familiar. She turned and saw Alonso beside her, smiling.

" I saw you striding down Alcala in a most determined way,"
he said. " I wondered what you were being so purposeful about,
so I followed. You simply took a tram, and so here I am."

This was one of those tram stops where the conductor got
down and had a long talk with other conductors, so there was
plenty of time.

" But what were you doing here at this time ? " she said.
She had always imagined that when he wasn't with her he was
at home, especially since he was so broke, and she felt hurt to
think he might have been lunching with someone else.

" Oh, I was in Baviera with some friends. You're going to
meet them this evening."

The conductor climbed back lethargically into the tram.

" I must get out," said Alonso, " this doesn't go my way."
He got up and smiled down at her. " Seven, in Baviera." He
went up to the conductor: " I wish to pay that young lady's
fare," and came back with her ticket. He waited until the tram
started, then jumped off and bowed to her. She saw him walk
off towards the metro station. He gave the impression that he
walked very slowly, but she knew from experience that it was
very difficult to keep up with him.

In Baviera that evening she found Rafael, Antonio and Jaime
standing at the bar. Rafael explained that they were so poor
now that they stood at the bar because there they didn't have to
give a tip. In spite of their poverty, they offered her a drink
which she accepted, as there was no sign of Alonso.

She asked them once more what they thought of the situation.
Rafael said everything would be all right. Jaime was silent, and
Antonio attacked the Communists. " They have no understanding of Spain," he said, " they don't know the first thing
about the Spanish character. It's so ridiculous to go burning
churches at a time like this. It's so pointless! So childish! "

" I don't believe the Communists did it," said Maria.

" Of course they did. Who else would ? "

" There are lots of people who would, simply to discredit the
Communists. After all, everyone always assumes it's them."

" They're like a lot of children. It makes me furious when
they do things like that."

" Are you a Catholic, then ? " asked Maria.

" No, I was brought up as one, but I'm not now. I'm a traditionalist, and it makes me sick to see these people trying to reorganise Spain without the slightest knowledge. Burning churches is just a demonstration of that. I like the church and I like churches, although I'm no longer a Catholic. It's an integral part of Spain's tradition."

" They probably know more about Spain than you think," said Maria, weakly. " What do you think ? " she asked Rafael.

Rafael smiled and pointed to his glass. " Don't ask me. I don't know anything. As long as the beer's good in Baviera, I'm happy."

" I've never seen Rafael unhappy in his life," said Antonio, " and that says very little for him."

Rafael smiled good naturedly. " It's nice to be happy."

" How is the church an integral part of Spain's tradition ? " said Maria, and then feeling she had let herself in for too much, added: " No, it would take too long to answer. I'd better ask you some other time."

" You know as much about Spanish history as I do," said Antonio, although he would have liked to go on. " I'd better not go into that now."

" Well," said Rafael, " I don't know anything, but if it's as traditional as you say, things like this won't affect it." He smiled, pleased to have made everything comfortable again.

Antonio laughed. " Perhaps they won't. Anyhow, the worst enemies of any tradition are the people who profess to believe in it. The worst enemies of the Church to-day are the clergy. At one time you know," he addressed himself only to Maria, " you used to get miracles and visions everywhere. In every village there was someone who'd seen the Virgin in one form or another—and so you got those names—Virgin of the Dove, Virgin of the Olive Tree, and so on. No one ever questioned them. Now the Church tries to be scientific and up to date, with the result that, if anyone sees the Virgin or performs a miracle, no one believes it unless there are the most rigid proofs. They expect a photographer and ten witnesses to be there." He threw up his hands in despair. " Superstition is so necessary!

Just imagine what the Gospels would be like if they were scientific and with illustrations—photographs of loaves and fishes before the miracle, loaves and fishes afterwards."

" I don't like superstition."

" It's so necessary. You can't think how necessary it is, especially to Spaniards. They're not materialists in any sense— even our Communists aren't really—that's why it's madness to go round preaching dialectical materialism here. Any cranky, mystic doctrine would be better." He gesticulated wildly with both hands. "And you know—a creed like dialectical materialism is more dangerous, its tyranny more thorough than feudalism or dictatorship, because it attacks one's whole attitude to life."

" So do dictators, and anyhow, I'm a materialist."

" No, they don't, they can't. Not in that way, and you're not a materialist. I can see that."

Maria shrugged her shoulders. " I am, besides the alternative to materialism isn't superstition."

" I didn't say it was, but I think superstition is important. I like it."

" I don't, I think it's pernicious."

" Why ? "

" Anything is which blinds people to the truth."

" The truth! The truth! " He gave an exasperated sigh and banged the counter. " What on earth do people mean by the truth ? "

" Oh," said Maria, " it's impossible to argue with you. You don't let one assume anything. Surely you admit some things are truer than others."

" No, I don't. There is one kind of fact and another—one balances them—the result is not truth. It is a solution which differs for everyone."

" One must assume something. Otherwise every judgment becomes irrelevant. You can't think in a vacuum."

" It's very complicated," said Antonio, " we must go into it sometime. I'm sorry you're a Communist. It's a mistake."

" I'm not a Communist, but I sympathise with them." She saw Alonso come in with two men she had not met. " Here's Alonso."

Alonso and his companions came over to the bar. They all knew the others. "This is Fuentes," said Alonso, pushing forward a small man with a young but wrinkled monkey face, "and this is Hereda." He indicated a tall, fair man in a blue blazer who looked English, like an Edwardian cricketer. He had light hazel eyes and a reddish moustache.

Maria shook hands with them. They exchanged a few words with Antonio and his friends and then went off to a table.

"I'm sure you're confused," said Maria to Antonio before she left him, "and I'll think of something in a minute to show you what I mean."

"It's impossible not to be confused." He bowed gloomily as she left.

Hereda and Fuentes were in very high spirits. They laughed a lot at nothing at all and had a great many private jokes which were meaningless to everyone else, but at which Alonso smiled indulgently. He stopped them after a short time in order to present them properly to Maria. "Hereda was a painter," he said, "but now he's a journalist, and Fuentes is a lawyer."

"I wouldn't have thought either of them were that," said Maria.

Fuentes and Hereda laughed uproariously. "We don't look our parts," said Fuentes. "It's better not to."

"Neither does Alonso," said Hereda. "He looks like a business man."

"A stockbroker."

"A Señorito."

"No. He's not at all a Señorito," said Maria indignantly.

"I haven't got that kind of good looks," said Alonso.

"What do you think of the political situation?" asked Maria.

This made them explode again. "Politics," said Hereda. "Politics!"

"We think of nothing else," said Fuentes.

"Our whole life is politics."

Maria stopped listening. Their constant bursts of laughter and their manner made her feel they treated everyone as a joke.

9

The following day Alonso had made up his mind to leave for San Sebastian as soon as possible. The cook had told his father that he had borrowed from the housekeeping money, and the old man was outraged. He met Maria in the morning, worried but determined.

" I'm taking the night train to-day, I've phoned San Sebastian and the sitter says I can start to-morrow. I'll do it in a week."

She tried to make him change his mind with no success. She declared she would have to spend her usual time at the library whether he was leaving that night or not.

" At least come with me to the station this evening. I'll pay your taxi fare back."

" I don't want my taxi fare."

" Will you come to the station ? "

" No."

However, in the evening he called for her in a taxi, and pleaded with her in the passage of the Pension not to be furious.

" Well, if I go to the station with you," she said, " I must let them know when I'll be back for dinner."

" You won't be in to dinner. You'll have it with me."

" Then you'll miss your train."

" I've decided not to go to-night after all. I can't leave you like this."

In the taxi he told her: " I'll spend the night in a hotel and leave first thing in the morning. I only hope my family doesn't find out."

After a meal at the German restaurant, they went on to La Granja. If something unpleasant had to be done, Maria was all for getting it over at once, and would far rather he had gone on the night train, because he would be back sooner. A week without Alonso seemed inexpressibly boring and flat, just library and Pension, Pension and library. Half-heartedly they argued with each other, knowing perfectly well that Alonso could not stop Maria being resentful about his departure, and she could not stop him from going. They drank a lot, hoping that would cheer them. Time went by, precious time which she thought he could have spent far better on the train, while their spirits sank lower and lower.

"I'm only going to get some money for *your* sake," he kept repeating, "so that your last week in Spain can be tremendous."

At last, turning round to look for the waiter, he saw a young man near their table and sprang up. "It's Ignacio," he exclaimed, "I'll bring him over."

Ignacio's appearance was not prepossessing, short and stocky, mousy-haired and with a greyish skin. He had the face of a malnourished child, his uncombed hair stood on end, he wore thick tortoiseshell-rimmed glasses which made his eyes look tiny and almost blind, and he smiled madly, disclosing a row of large, prominent but unexpectedly white teeth. As he looked at Maria his smile became wider and wider, stretching from ear to ear. He squinted. "What a lovely girl," he said, spluttering excitedly. "A foreigner. Just the kind of girl I like."

Alonso reassured her. "It's all right. It's simply his kind of compliment."

"Well Alonso," said Ignacio, as he sat down beside Maria and stared at her. "Well Alonsito of my soul! Beloved Alonso?"

"Well?" said Alonso, good naturedly.

"Well? Well nothing?" Still eyeing Maria, Ignacio exploded.

She smiled, bewildered. Ignacio turned right round and stared all the harder, whistled, said "lovely girl!" and winked at Alonso.

"What'll you drink?" said Alonso.

"Water," Ignacio beamed, "I love water."

"Why?"

"It stops me being thirsty."

"Don't you like alcohol?" asked Alonso.

"Yes. Not now, though. I don't really like it." He was no longer smiling, but looked at them with a childish seriousness. "I think water's got a much nicer taste, really."

Alonso ordered some water. "And bring three glasses," said Ignacio to the waiter. "It will be so wonderful to think I made Alonso drink water. You will, won't you?"

"Yes."

" And you will, too ? "

" Yes," said Maria.

" Hurrah! " said Ignacio.

" It's nothing out of the ordinary," said Maria. " We often drink water."

" Is she your girl ? " said Ignacio.

" Yes," said Alonso, and smiled at Maria. " Are you ? "

" It depends on what that means."

" Oh, you know what it means," said Ignacio.

" It might mean anything. I don't know," said Maria.

" You must know," said Ignacio. " If you are his girl you must know, so if you don't know, you're not his girl."

The water and three glasses arrived. Ignacio seized the jug and began to pour out the water.

" He's a surrealist," said Alonso to Maria.

" Not a surrealist," said Ignacio, and stopped pouring until he had made it quite clear. " A superrealist."

" What's the difference ? "

" It's a difference of degree." He went on pouring, a little in one glass and then in another, keeping them even. He concentrated very hard on this, and when they were practically full, looked up. " Now comes the interesting part," he said, " I'll just do one at a time." He filled the glass nearest to him right to the brim and then began to add water to it, drop by drop. " Watch," he said, " the water will curve right out of the glass before it overflows."

They had to lower their heads until they were almost lying on the table, to get a profile view of the water. Each drop might now be the last, and no one knew how far the upward curve would swell before it started to run down the sides of the glass on to the table.

" Let me try," said Maria, and took over the jug. She was clumsier than Ignacio, and instead of a drop, let out a thin stream which destroyed the curve and made a mess of the table. Fortunately, the table had a marble top. " Had we better wipe it up ? " she said.

" Oh no," said Ignacio, " let's try the next one."

This one was more successful, and Ignacio judged the quantity so exactly that he could shake the table lightly, making the shape of the curve alter as the water moved from side to side, without one drop overflowing. They watched it for some time, until Ignacio decided there was no more to be got out of it. "That's that," he said, laughing, and poured some water on, making a far worse mess of the table than Maria had done.

Alonso did the third glass and was no more successful than Maria, though he controlled the jug better. After that, the table was covered with water and some was dripping on to the floor.

The waiter came up and began to grumble about the water. He seemed more annoyed with Ignacio than with the others, probably because Ignacio grinned at him irresponsibly all the time as though it were all a joke.

"We were looking at the curve of the water," said Ignacio, "it was very nice."

The waiter said nothing but mopped up the pool on the table. "It's gone on to the floor," he said angrily when he had finished.

"Don't bother about that," said Ignacio, "It'll dry by itself in this warm atmosphere."

"We were just on the point of leaving when you came," said Alonso.

"I think we'd better be going." He looked at Maria.

"Yes," said Maria, and so as not to seem rude to Ignacio, "as you've got to do all your packing to-night."

"Is he going away?" said Ignacio.

"Yes, to San Sebastian to-morrow morning."

They left a large tip for the waiter, Ignacio paying most of it. He was upset to have annoyed the waiter so much, and insisted that he could have made it better by explaining. He left with them and said he had better go and get some sleep, he had arrived from Paris that morning.

Just outside the door he said goodbye to them and whispered loudly to Maria, "As he's going you can be my girl."

"When are you leaving?" said Alonso.

"In a few days."

"I shan't see you again, then."

"No."

" Come and see me in San Sebastian on your way back."

" I don't think I shall be able to," said Ignacio, " but if I can, I shall." He shook hands with both of them and hurried off.

After they had walked a little way down the road, he came running after them. " What's her address ? " he said to Alonso.

Alonso gave him the name of Maria's Pension. " What do you want it for ? "

" I want to see her again, and I shouldn't be able to if I didn't know her address." He hurried off again.

10

After Ignacio had left them, they went for a long walk, up to the Puerta del Sol and round it three times until they chose which side street they should take. Then they walked aimlessly on, taking whichever turning looked inviting to Maria. She made all the decisions and, not knowing her way about, led them back twice to the Puerta del Sol from which they had started. She turned down another street, determined not to get back there a third time.

The streets were badly lit by lamps, bracketed out from the walls and far away from each other, so that the heavy iron bars over the windows cast long shadows which stretched across the walls, and where they were equidistant from two lamps, cast a pale shadow on either side.

Alonso held Maria's hand all the time, and once stopped under a lamp, looked at her, kissed her, not with his usual deliberateness, but tentatively. " How angry are you, Marichu ? "

" I'm not angry." She was embarrassed to see him without his usual self-assurance.

It was cold and there were very few people walking about. This part of Madrid was neither wholly rich nor working class; affluent blocks of flats stood side by side with the most dilapidated, wretched houses. The small tascas which they passed were full and animated.

After taking two turnings to the right and one to the left to keep away from their starting point, Maria hesitated whether to go straight on, which might lead too far from the centre of the town, or whether to turn once more. " I don't want to go back to the Puerta del Sol again," she said, " I feel almost superstitious about it. Let's go in a completely new direction."

" In the direction of the Retiro ? "

" Yes, that would be nice."

Alonso took over control, and they walked on silently. Maria had no idea where she was, but she saw that Alonso knew his way about Madrid perfectly. They went down streets she had never seen before, some of them very narrow and irregular. They walked quickly to keep warm.

Alonso was going to the Retiro in a very roundabout way, he explained. When they reached it, Maria allowed herself to feel exhausted, and freeing her hand she slipped her arm through his. He pressed it to his side and smiled at her. They walked on more slowly, away from the Gran Via, round the Retiro. " Are you tired ? " said Alonso.

" I don't know, but I want to go on walking."

After some time, they reached a wide road, without people or traffic, and with very few lighted windows. Suddenly they both saw something in the distance which looked like an enormous silver caterpillar winding quickly along towards them.

" What on earth's that ? " said Maria.

" I can't think."

They stood still and watched it, and Alonso kissed her hair. " It's coming towards us. We'll wait for it."

It moved quickly, but owing to the bad lighting, they didn't discover until it was a few yards away that it was a cyclist towing a row of shining, new bicycles. It was impossible to see how they were attached or how they kept up. They didn't move in a stiff, straight line, but exactly followed the route of the leading bicycle, whose rider, having the whole road to himself, advanced in a gentle zigzag.

When he was near enough, Alonso shouted: " What are they ?

What are they for ? "

The rider smiled at them and circled over to their side of the pavement. " Bicycles," he said, triumphantly, " bicycles."

" Nice new ones," said Alonso.

" Yes, Señor, brand new." He smiled to see them mystified, and circled away. Encouraged by their attention, he bent over the handle-bars, pedalled hard, zigzagged more wildly, making his shining train perform like acrobats. He could not stay near them very long unless he turned round, and that was impossible, so after one or two more hairpin turns, he waved goodbye to them and sped away. His course was downhill, and he stopped pedalling, sat motionless and looked straight ahead. The row of bicycles behind him stopped waving, stiffened and became one twinkling line. The light caught the turning bars of the wheels and the tyres rolled softly over the road making a sound like a loud, muffled, high-pitched purr.

Maria and Alonso watched them until they reached the bottom of the road and curved boldly round a corner.

" He should have been much younger," said Alonso (the rider was middle-aged and solidly built), " very young, slender and handsome."

" He was very graceful all the same."

The journey back to Alcala seemed interminable. Maria's feet were frozen and half numb, and she kept taking her hands out of her pockets to rub them and blow on them. Alonso put his warm hand into her pocket and gently massaged her fingers.

Back in La Granja they drank beer. It was a bad choice, a cold and unstimulating drink. After a quarter of an hour or so, Alonso declared that the atmosphere was uncongenial, and said he must think of somewhere gayer, where one could stay up really late, till four in the morning.

" But I shall fall asleep long before then," said Maria.

" No. You'll get sleepy between half-past one and half-past two, but after that you'll revive, and by four o'clock it will be wonderful. You'll feel like going for another walk."

It was a cloudless night, and the sky was full of stars. The air was so cold that they could see their breath as small clouds. The sound of people talking and laughing on the other side of the street came over to them.

He kissed her cheek. " Now I feel so happy. Being out here after the café, after our quarrel, after the whole of this evening, has a wonderful dryness. It's the sort of dryness you feel after tears or a scene. There is no moisture hidden anywhere. It has all come out and been dispersed."

They walked on very slowly. He had not yet made up his mind where they were going. He stopped in a doorway, put his arms round her and lay his head on her shoulder. His cheek warmed her neck.

" I don't need to do anything at all when I'm with you," said Maria, " It's all done for me. The reconciliation was the man with the bicycles."

" The whole world, at least the whole of Madrid, is simply the expression, the agent of our moods. I'm glad you realise that." He spoke confidentially into her ear. " But only when we're together, you see. When I'm alone, they have no relation to my mood at all."

11

They ended up at a club, a warm place, and for the first hour there were two singers and two guitarists. They did not do real flamenco, but Americanised versions of Andalusian songs and hackneyed tangos and paso-dobles. Alonso was glad of the music such as it was, because he didn't feel like talking.

After two glasses of whisky, he dozed, smiling happily, his head resting on the back of the seat, his hand in Maria's. She fell into a coma with her eyes open.

How long they remained like that they didn't know, but later when they revived, they found that most of the other people had left. Alonso drank some more whisky and became animated. He pointed out to Maria a typical business man who was sitting holding both the hands of a young lady and looking at her tearfully. As he pointed him out, he imitated him.

Maria was not properly awake, and he pinched her arm. " What do you want to talk about ? " he said.

" Anything."

" All right, I feel like some poetry," he said, " poetry about love and the Spring."

" It's more like winter than Spring."

" Never mind:

'O amada mia! Es el dulce
tiempo de la primavera.'

" Where's that from ? "

" Ruben Dario." He repeated the lines and some of the first verse of the Primaveral. " It's not what I want, really."

He thought for a moment and then recited the beginning of Gongora's " Del Palacio de la Primavera." He rolled the words on his tongue, and when he had finished, sighed with satisfaction. He began to talk to Maria about Gongora, telling her to wake up from time to time. " You shouldn't like him," he said. " Do you know what he called your Queen Elizabeth ? " He quoted the lines from the " Spanish Armada."

Maria was surprised and frightened by Alonso's unsuspected erudition, and became more and more silent. He began to explain why he liked Gongora so much. " By writing in an archaic idiom, drawing on Greek and Roman literature, he found a way of being just as much a seventeenth century figure as Lope, in fact, more. One verse of his to some Duke, one line of the Soledades, gives me a more powerful impression of that time than anything written by his obviously up-to-date contemporaries. He interpreted the world around him by creating a complete and fantastic world of his own. I feel such sympathy for people like that. People who are wholly aware live partly in the past. I'm sure of that."

" You always looked so bored when I talked about Spanish literature. You always pretended you didn't know anything about it until to-night. That was sly of you. I must have seemed very silly, lecturing you on things I knew less about than you. I wish I had your knowledge."

D*

He kissed her cheek, his eyes were shining and he was very flushed. " It isn't that you haven't got knowledge, but it's got a bit stuck. All your knowledge of the Cid and the Golden Age is there in your little head," he tapped the place where he imagined it to be, " lying there, waiting to be taken out and exhibited when you write a long, long thesis. It goes on piling up and sometimes it gets a bit bulky, and then you spend a short time tidying it up, and that process of tidying you call a piece of original criticism, I think, don't you ? " He didn't wait for her to answer. " It's a process which you'll be able to go through more and more easily, and your aim is to get it so beautifully taped that you can do it without thinking. By that time you'll be ripe for your fifth thesis. How well I can imagine it." He laughed at her. " Possible sources in a recently discovered play by Lope de Vega. Footnote 1. We (that is, Marichu, darling Marichu whom Alonso loves so much—but, of course, by then she'll have put all that kind of thing behind her) find that both Lope and Señor X (a possible source) use the word ' because ' frequently in the same context. See notes 18 and 20, pages, etc. It's a delicious occupation, but you must see that it's in no way an experience, except in the way that a crossword puzzle is."

They walked up and down Eduardo Dato, where her Pension was, unable to make up their minds to separate. Alonso recited again :

> " O amada mia! Es el dulce
> tiempo de la Primavera "

and again Maria said it was more like winter.

He stopped and kissed her. " You must reassure me before I go away. Do you like me as much as ever ? "

" Yes, quite as much."

" Not more ? "

" More, much more." She felt, as she had felt earlier in the evening, embarrassed by his anxiety and laughed nervously. " Still, you don't care about anything."

" I know, but I like to have what I can. I want you to go on liking me."

When they reached the door of the Pension, they had to wait

for some time before the sereno came with the keys to let her in. Alonso clapped twice for him, but he was right at the other end of the street.

" Would you like to marry me ? " he said, suddenly.

" No.   You wouldn't like it either."

" It would be a way of keeping you in Madrid."

" When I'm able to, I shall stay in Madrid anyhow. What time is it do you think ? "

" About three." He looked at her. " Marichu, there's nothing the matter, is there ? "

She looked at him, his eyes were moist and his forehead was wrinkled. " Of course there's nothing the matter. What could be the matter ? "

" I might bore you."

" You couldn't."

The sereno approached, rattling his keys and puffing. He was a bad tempered old man, which was not surprising, because he had the most tiring and unpleasant job. He had rebuked them once before for clapping several times impatiently instead of waiting, after clapping once, until he came. He said he could always hear, one clap was enough.

" Well, goodbye, Marichu," said Alonso, kissing her cheek. " Don't bother about the sereno.   I'll tip him."

" Goodbye."

" And please write."

" I shall."

" Is there anything the matter ? "

" There isn't, really there isn't. Perhaps you're beginning to have a hangover after all that whisky."

They exchanged good evenings with the sereno. " Good morning more like it," he said.

" Well, good morning, then," said Alonso.

The sereno opened the door shakily with a large key. Maria went in and waved goodbye to Alonso from the passage. The front door was made of glass. She could see he was still looking in at her and went back towards the door. He flattened his nose against the glass and smiled.

12

Maria was woken from a deep sleep at eleven o'clock the next morning by the maid. " The telephone."

" Oh, say I'm asleep," said Maria.

" I did, but they didn't take any notice."

Maria flung on her dressing gown, tired and angry, and went to the phone. It was Ignacio.

" Hullo," he said in his hiccoughing voice, " Maria ? "

" Yes. I was asleep."

" Can I see you ? "

" Not now. I'm going to sleep for a long time."

" This evening ? "

" All right."

" Good. At La Granja ? "

" Yes."

" At eight, then. There'll be a lot of us."

" How do you mean, a lot of you ? "

" Oh, you know—the others'll be there." He seemed to find this funny and chuckled.

" All right, then," said Maria, " I'm going back to bed now," and put down the receiver. She found the maid and told her not to disturb her on any condition—not even for lunch—and went to sleep again in ten minutes.

When she woke up it was about half-past three. Everything was quiet and there was no one about in the Pension. She went to the library and tried to work. Padre Moreno was not there that afternoon. " He had to go and give a lesson," the caretaker explained to her, as though she had a right to know why he hadn't come.

After wading through the position of the church in the days of the Cid, and making a few illegible notes, she tidied her handsome desk and left the library.

" A lot of work to-day," said the caretaker, approvingly, as he let her out.

" Not as much as there ought to be."

" Oh Señorita, you're too severe with yourself."

She walked the whole way, past the statue of Christopher

Columbus, down the Castellana, past the Biblioteca Nacional, the Correos, to Baviera. It was now half-past seven.

In Baviera there were several of Alonso's friends, Antonio, Rafael and Jaime. Most of the other people there were fat, blonde Germans. She sat down in the corner and ordered a manzanilla. Rafael waved to her and then came over. " And where's Alonso ? " he said, blue-eyed and smiling.

" In San Sebastian."

" Really ? "

" Yes. He went to paint a portrait."

Rafael beckoned to the other two to come over and told them the news. He looked fresher and pinker than ever and never stopped smiling. Antonio and Jaime did not look so cheerful.

" I've been correcting exercises," said Antonio, and opened his case, taking out some exercise books. " Look! " He pointed proudly to the red ink lines he had made, " they're nice and straight, aren't they ? "

" Yes, they're lovely," said Maria.

" I like bad exercises," said Antonio, " because then I can make a lot of corrections." He found one and showed it to her. The page was so covered with lines and comments in red ink that one could hardly see the writing underneath. " That one's the best."

" It would take a lot of beating."

" One must enjoy something about it," he said, sadly, " otherwise it would be unbearable."

Antonio was soon riding his hobby horse once more. " I must explain my position more fully to you some time," he said. " I'm not so muddled as you think. You must understand that the classless society, the vision of enormous machines being worked by everyone for everyone's good, and by good I mean simply a standard of comfort, the abandoning of every kind of standard of taste which, after all, is inextricably bound up with the class system, seems awful to me. On the other hand, I am prepared to admit that at the present time everything is awful, money and power are in the hands of vulgarians, taste has deteriorated, and I agree with you that something must be done. But you'd hand power over to the workers and that would be fatal—they're as bad, worse, than the people you'd taken it from—they've been educated by them. You would get more of those super cinemas, more of those super cafés everywhere— you can imagine what it would be like."

"Anyhow, Alonso likes those cafés," said Maria, "and he's not a worker."

"Yes, but he likes them in such a superior way. He laughs at them. He enjoys their vulgarity. It's quite different from the way in which your workers, say, would like them."

"You can't base a political theory on an awful vision of super cinemas and cafés," said Maria.

"I don't see why not, if other people can base it on a vision of economics or a pile of statistics. It's no more abstract."

At eight o'clock, Maria left them and made her way across the road to La Granja. It was a move from the right wing to the left wing, for when she arrived, Ignacio was in full swing, stammering, hiccoughing, gurgling the reasons why Super-realists were Communists. Sitting with him were Fuentes and Hereda and a young man Maria didn't know. They were all excited, and had probably been drinking for some time. Ignacio looked up at her through his thick spectacles and smiled madly.

"Here's Maria," he said, loudly. "Who do you know?"

"Everyone, I think, except. . . ." She looked at the young man she didn't know.

"Oh, that's Perez. He's a bullfighter."

"A fine bullfighter," laughed Fuentes.

"A Superrealist bullfighter," said Hereda. "He's entirely on the side of the bull. That's why he doesn't get on."

"I do get on," said Perez, indignantly." "No one does more than novilladas at my age, but," he added, proudly, "I *am* a Superrealist."

Maria was still standing. She looked round for a chair and Ignacio saw her. "She hasn't got a chair," he exploded, and they all leapt up and offered theirs. She took the nearest one, which happened to be Hereda's, and he went to get one from another table.

Ignacio ordered a glass of manzanilla for her and another for himself. He hadn't finished the one he had, but he told the waiter that he liked to see a lot of glasses on the table. Then he ordered some more for everyone, and when they protested, saying they hadn't enough money, took out a thick wad of hundred peseta notes from his pocket and smiled at them childishly. He then put the notes on the table and took out of his pockets a pencil, a penknife, some ten centimo pieces, a passport photograph and some string. He laid them all neatly in front of him. " These are my resources,"he said. " How I like to see a table covered with things. In my studio in Paris all the tables are covered with things. It looks very pretty."

The others emptied their pockets on to the table and admired the effect. " What about you ? " said Hereda to Maria.

" I think perhaps there's enough," said Maria, cautiously.

" Perhaps there is," said Perez, fastidiously, " perhaps a little too much. I think that envelope is wrong."

" You're right. You're absolutely right," said Ignacio, and removed the envelope and put it in his pocket, although it didn't belong to him. " It makes all the difference."

They looked at the table critically for some time, moving an object here and there. The waiter looked on unconcerned, used to anything in La Granja. A few people at the other tables abandoned their dominoes or ludo for a moment to have a look.

" They're all going off to have supper soon," said Ignacio. " I said we wouldn't go with them. We'll have supper by ourselves. But we'll all meet afterwards." He looked at Maria, his eyes more crossed than ever, and made fantastically small by his thick glasses, and she wondered if he was planning some Marx brother assault on her. He was capable of anything.

" All right," she said, uncertainly.

" Do you realise what day it is ? " said Hereda.

" I do," said Perez, " the feast of . . . let me think."

" No," said Hereda, scornfully, " nothing like that. The anniversary of Primo de Rivera."

" Christ! " said Ignacio. " To think I hadn't thought of that."

" Well, we must do something about it."

" Yes, we must."

They decided to think of what to do during supper. They

finished their drinks, removed their property from the table and went off to discuss it. "We'll have thought of something," said Hereda. "You needn't worry."

The fears Maria had of Ignacio were quite unfounded. He took her to a very nice restaurant and told her he wanted to talk to her about Alonso. He started off by talking about himself and his life in Paris. He disapproved of the café existence he was leading at the moment, and said he could only stand a few days of that while he was on holiday. In Paris he hardly ever went to a café or saw anyone, but painted as long as the light would allow him and drew after that. He wanted to be a great painter.

They did not get to Alonso until the end of supper, when Ignacio, after describing a nice girl he had had and who had left him, suddenly turned to Maria and said, "I'm very worried about Alonso."

"Why?"

"He's not a good painter. He's not at all a good painter."

"Well, it doesn't matter. He knows he isn't and he doesn't mind."

"He doesn't know he isn't, he says he isn't. He thinks he's a good painter really, but he's having a lazy spell. He thinks he's bad at the moment because he's lazy, but do you know how long the lazy spell has lasted? Ever since he was nineteen."

"I think he knows all that."

"Every time I see him he says he's going to Paris for a year. He's been saying that for years now. About four years ago I persuaded him to go to Paris. I found a studio for him and fixed the date. He kept putting it off. . . Have you ever seen any of his work?"

"Yes."

"Well, it's dreadful."

"I've only seen a portrait he did of me and a sketch he did of a cat. They weren't very good, I know."

"And he really had talent. He was one of the most talented people I've ever met." He waved his hands as he spoke. "And now all he does is paint portraits, bad portraits."

"I still don't see that it matters," said Maria, loyally.

Ignacio was angry. " Why not ? "

" Well, he's contented."

" A painter who's contented to be a fifth rate painter, when he has the knowledge of what good painting is that Alonso has is a contradiction in terms, it doesn't exist. Can't you see that ? "

" Perhaps. I don't know anything about painting," said Maria weakly, and added, stupidly, " I daresay it was a mistake to do Popeye."

" I'm not talking about that," said Ignacio, crushingly. " You don't have to have any knowledge of painting to understand what I mean. Popeye doesn't matter. It was a commercial proposition and it only lasted a month or two. If I was offered something like that I might take it. It's not at all important. But these portraits don't bring in any money, a miserable amount. I know he says he does them to make money, but that's just a way of justifying himself. He doesn't believe it really and I certainly don't. He doesn't need the money."

" Yes he does."

" If he was really serious he wouldn't mind about that. His family would support him. They do now. His father's very generous to him. All his reasons are absurd. They're an excuse for him to go on doing something he doesn't take seriously, something which is bounded by the taste of his sitters, so that he won't have time to do anything else."

" He told me he didn't want to do much. He said he didn't like doing the portraits he did, and he simply wanted to do franker ones—I'm not sure about that, because it was two years ago."

" It doesn't make any difference what he said," said Ignacio. He no longer looked mad, but calmly passionate. " The point is, as I said, a painter like that is a contradiction. He's not a fool and he's not as flippant as he'd like to be and, therefore, he must be extremely unhappy."

" I don't think he is." It was a shock to her to find that Alonso whom she had always thought to be above and beyond any but her criticism, who managed to remain so elusive, no matter how much one saw of him, could be considered an unhappy failure by someone else. " To be a good painter isn't

everything," she said. "People exist apart from their painting
or whatever they do. As a person, he's absolutely successful.
He's interested in everything. He's never bored. He's alive to
everything."

"I wouldn't say that. His interest in things is limited. He
dramatises his own position so much."

"He doesn't, he's the most natural person."

"Yes, he does. He sees himself as a sort of amused spectator."

"It's no use expecting me to agree with you," said Maria,
firmly. "I think you're quite wrong about him."

Ignacio ignored this and her implied plea that he should stop
his criticisms. "I never thought that the serious young painter
of nineteen that I knew would grow up into this settled semi-
drunken poseur."

"Oh, he's not a poseur." She paused for a moment in her
indignation. "How could he be? There's no one he wants to
pose to. He doesn't want to impress anyone."

"He wants to impress himself. There's something very
wrong with him now."

"There's something wrong with all of us."

"Oh no, there's nothing wrong with me."

Maria was silent. She was trying to think of what was wrong
with Ignacio, but it was all so obvious that it couldn't be very
important. He clearly wasn't as mad as he had seemed to be,
and knew very well what he was about.

"I like him," said Ignacio. "I used to like him very much.
Otherwise I wouldn't be concerned about him."

"Why did you want to talk to me about him?"

"I want you to help me to persuade him to go to Paris."

"I can't do that. He hates people interfering, and I don't
think one should."

"Don't be silly," said Ignacio. "You can't go taking his
word for everything he feels like that. He ought to be persuaded,
whether he likes it or not."

"I don't believe one should ever persuade anyone else to do
anything." All the same, she knew that she was always trying
to persuade Alonso to do things.

13

They found the others in a tasca. As soon as they joined them, Ignacio changed quite naturally. He beamed at them and asked them excitedly, " What did you decide ? "

" We're going to the Cemetery of San Isidoro," said Hereda.

" That's where he was buried," he explained to Maria, " and we'll wait for his ghost."

" We'll insult it," said Fuentes.

" It's high time someone told him what they think of him," said Perez.

" Of course," said Ignacio.

" We know what we're going to say, too," said Fuentes.

" We're prepared for his answers," said Perez.

" We can't go yet, it's not late enough," said Ignacio. " What shall we do now ? "

" Go to a café."

" To Chicote, the haunt of the Señoritos."

They went out of the tasca where they had been having dinner, whistling. Perez to show what a fine bullfighter he was, did an excellent mariposa with an imaginary cape and bull.

" That's my paso doble they're whistling," he said to Maria, " every torero has his paso doble, you know, and when you excel, the band plays it."

" I know," said Maria, " and one famous bullfighter never had one written for him. I always thought that sad."

" He can't have wanted one," said Perez, proudly. " Most musicians would be only too glad to write a paso doble for a torero. Then they're sure of their work being played."

They walked down the street in great disorder, Hereda and Fuentes leading the way, whistling and gesticulating whenever they passed a pretty girl, Perez on his own, still bullfighting, and Maria following at a distance soberly with Ignacio.

When they reached Chicote, Hereda and Fuentes waited for the others to catch them up. When they were all assembled outside the door of the café, they stepped back gallantly and asked Maria to go in first. She did so, and was surprised to see Fuentes and Perez rush past her, right down to the other end of the café, where a solid bourgeois couple and their son were slowly approaching a table. Fuentes and Perez neatly slipped into the chairs and leant over the table as though they had been there for some time. The couple stood still, indignant and surprised. By the time Maria, Ignacio and Hereda arrived, they were protesting loudly.

" This is our table," said the man.

" How were we to know ? " said Perez, innocently. " We got here and sat down, and now you say this is your table."

" I suppose one can go up to anyone and say the table they happen to be sitting at is yours," said Fuentes. " I hadn't thought of that."

" You saw us walking to this table," said the woman, " you must have done. We were about a metre away when you sat down here."

" Ah yes, now I remember," said Perez, " I did see someone standing near here. I thought they were leaving. It must have been you," he turned to them delightedly, " it must have been."

" So it must," said Fuentes, " how amazing. But would you have said it was a metre ? I'd have put it at more, although I don't want anyone to think I have anything but the greatest respect for the Señora's powers of calculation."

" About a metre and a half," said Perez. He looked up at the now furious family. " What do you think ? "

" One metre and six centimetres, to be exact, " said Hereda, sitting down with the others.

The family looked about desperately for witnesses, but there was no one sitting very near (which made the seizure of that particular table even worse), and the waiter, smiling, said he had seen nothing. Maria didn't know whether to sit down or not.

Fuentes rose and addressed the family respectfully: " Señora, as you like this table so much, please take it from us as a mark of our respect." The others rose and bowed.

" Certainly not," said the woman, and the whole family began to move away.

" Or do us the honour of sitting here with us," went on Fuentes, unperturbed. " We can get some more chairs." As the family made no reply, but pursued its dignified course to a fairly distant table, he sat down and shrugged his shoulders. The others also sat down. " A pity! " sighed Fuentes, " such charming people."

" Charming, delicious," said Hereda.　" Didn't you think they were delightful ? " he asked Maria. He was not smiling, they none of them were.

" Yes," said Maria, " I did."

" Are we all going to drink cognac ? " asked Ignacio.

" If you pay for it."

" All right." Ignacio ordered.

A group of smart young men came in and sat down at a table near them.

" Señoritos," said Perez, excitedly.

" What nice suits! " said Fuentes in a loud voice.

" Very nicely turned out," said Hereda, " they're like advertisements."

" What a lot of Señoritos there are," said Maria, " every café's full of them."

" When the time comes," said Perez, " you'll find there are more of us."

" That's right," said Fuentes, his monkey face screwed up with delight. " Let's give them something to think about, let's talk about the revolution."

Perez started. He might have been imitating Pepe because he banged the table with his fist and frowned in true mock revolutionary style. " We've got it all prepared," he said with emphasis. " Our plans are finished. We must wait till the Autumn."

" Then we burn the crops," said Hereda.

" Burn all the fincas of the big landowners—not *all* the crops," said Fuentes.

" Seize the banks," said Ignacio.

" Seize everything," said Maria, surprised at herself.

" Everything," said Perez, approvingly. " That's right. How right she is."

" The churches," said Ignacio, " they must be burnt down, I suppose."

" Oh, I'm sick of them," said Perez.

" Yes, we'll leave them out for a change," said Fuentes.

" You must remember they're Fascist arsenals," said Maria.

" How well she knows her facts," beamed Ignacio.

They drank up their cognac and ordered some more. Maria felt exalted after all the drink she had had, and smiled at everyone.

Hereda leant over to her and said, " But, frankly, don't you think the Señoritos handsome ? "

" No," she said, emphatically, " I've never admired them."

" Who ? " said Perez.

" The Señoritos."

The Señoritos couldn't help hearing, but they pretended not to listen. Hereda looked straight at their smiling faces. " They look like film stars."

" Like dummies in a shop window."

" How beautifully they do their hair."

" They're wonderfully clean."

" Spotless."

" When the revolution comes," said Fuentes, " we'll stand them in the shop windows and make them smile all day."

" In the evening," said Fuentes, " they'll have a shampoo and be packed off to bed."

" In the morning they'll have a manicure, a bath and do their hair beautifully," said Perez.

" They'll hardly notice the change."

" They won't notice it at all."

" We must preserve them like the pictures in the Prado."

" Perhaps they'll fight," said Maria.

" Oh no they won't—not the Señoritos." Perez' eyes were shining, and he looked at the other table, trying to provoke them to retaliate. The Señoritos went on talking to each other a little unconvincingly.

There was no knowing what Perez would do next. " I know the type that will fight," she said quickly, " though, of course, he's not a Señorito—that's Antonio."

" Which Antonio ? "

" The one who goes to Baviera."

" Yes, he'll fight."

" He should have been an Anarchist," said Fuentes.

" I like him," said Maria, " one can't dislike all Fascists."

" I don't dislike them," said Fuentes, and added with a melting glance at the other table, " and as for the Señoritos—I love them."

" I always had a weakness for Primo," said Hereda.

Ignacio had not been listening for some time and was playing with a piece of string, but he pricked up his ears at the mention of Primo. " It'll soon be time to go and see him."

" Let's leave here, anyhow," said Perez, " we might walk about for a bit."

Ignacio paid the bill and they went out in single file, Perez giving a sudden lurch as he passed the Señoritos' table, almost upsetting the chair of one of them and saying an insolent, " Excuse me."

They walked down the street aimlessly until they heard the sound of a harmonium. They looked for it and found it in a side street. An old woman was playing the wheezy instrument. They went over and listened to her.

" Can you play the International ? " said Perez.

" Yes," she said, " I can play anything I've heard once. I do it by ear."

" All right," he said, and gave her five pesetas.

She played it and they all sang except Maria. When it was finished, they asked the old woman to play it again. She did so, reluctantly, and this time they sang louder. A small crowd gathered near them, and Maria saw, or imagined she saw, some menacing Fascists on the pavement opposite. She began to be afraid. " I'm not going to wait," she said to Ignacio, and walked away.

He ran after her, " All right, I'll go with you. When this is over we can join the others."

When the noise died down, they walked back again. " We mustn't lose them," said Ignacio.

" I'm not going to the cemetery," said Maria.

" Why not ? "

" I'm tired. I'm going home."

Hereda and Fuentes came running to meet them. " She

wouldn't play it any more," said Fuentes.

" Let's go to the cemetery," said Hereda.

" We'll get a taxi."

" Where's Perez ? "

They found him in a doorway, bullfighting by himself. He was very indifferent, and didn't mind whether he lost them or not. He showed more interest when they reminded him of the visit to Primo, came out of his doorway and joined them.

They walked along Alcala, Perez whistling his paso doble against Fuentes' International. They hailed a taxi.

" We want to go to the cemetery of San Isidoro."

" All right," said the driver, unperturbed.

They got in, Maria between Hereda and Ignacio, Fuentes and Perez on the collapsible seats in front of them.

" Let's sing," said Ignacio.

They sang " Rocio, O mi Rocio " loudly and passionately. With the exception of Ignacio, they had fine, strong voices. Ignacio croaked out of tune and stopped at once good naturedly when Perez told him he was ruining everything.

Maria took advantage of a pause between the verse, and the chorus (they were still near the Puerta del Sol). " Please put me down here," she said, " I'd like to go home."

They stopped the taxi by banging on the window. " Oh, look," said Perez, " lovely girls."

" Yes, they're gypsies, Andalusians," said Fuentes.

Two dark girls were standing on the pavement selling roses. When they saw the taxi stop so near them, the girls came over to it, holding out their flowers.

" Roses ? " they said, smiling. Perez had already opened the door of the taxi. " Yes." He jumped out.

" I want some, too," said Fuentes, and got out, too. They shut the door behind them.

Maria tried to get up, but Ignacio held her arm. " Don't go," he said.

" I want to."

" Stay until they come back with the roses. I'm sure they're for you."

" All right."

The other two were a long time. They stood on the pavement laughing and talking to the girls. Hereda banged on the window. "Hurry up."

Fuentes and Perez took no notice. Fuentes was holding the hand of one of the girls, Perez was doing passes and must be boasting to them of his talent as a bullfighter.

Hereda banged on the window again. They said goodbye affectionately to the girls, took their roses and came back to the taxi.

"Roses," said Perez, as he opened the door and threw two large bunches of red roses on to Maria's lap.

"Thank you," said Maria, and smelt them.

"More roses," said Fuentes, handing her two more bunches as he climbed in.

"They're lovely, said Maria. "Now I must get out."

"Don't you like them?" said Perez, sadly.

"Let me smell them," said Hereda.

"I do like them," said Maria, finding it difficult to move, covered with roses and sandwiched tightly between the two men.

"Good," said Perez, and banged on the window. The taxi moved on. They began to sing again, each taking a rose and putting it in his buttonhole. Ignacio put some roses in Maria's hair and behind her ears. When the song was finished, Hereda looked out of the window and said, "Rosa fresca, rosa fresca, tan garrida y con amor."

"We must do some sayetas on roses," said Perez. "You start, Hereda."

"Red rose," sang Hereda in a high falsetto with the complicated wailing and trills of the canto jondo, "in the dark night you are black."

"Red rose," sang Perez next, "you lurk in the dark depths of that which bears us to the place of death."

"Ay! You will fade in the morning," was Fuentes.

Ignacio couldn't sing, so he recited. "It has been decided by small groups in taxis that roses shall be worn when visiting ghosts."

14

The taxi stopped outside the cemetery and they got out, Maria holding the roses unsteadily.

" Shall I wait ? " asked the driver.

" No," said Hereda.

" How will we get back ? " asked Maria, anxiously.

" We can walk for a bit and then get a tram as far as the Puerta del Sol."

The driver was reluctant to leave them, curious to see what they would do, and circled slowly round the street twice before going back towards the city.

They were on the outskirts of Madrid, beyond the working class suburb. It was a moonlit night. The high white walls of the cemetery were pale and gleaming, and behind them towered dark cypresses. There was only the sound of their feet as they walked towards the gate. Their excitement was solemn now and no one spoke. Maria was careful to stay by Ignacio. She had never imagined the time would come when she would turn to him as a person of sense and responsibility.

A carabinero suddenly appeared in front of the gate. He might have been a ghost, he made no sound and his pallor was a light green in the moonlight. He smiled slowly and displayed a mouthful of shining teeth. They had all been covered with gold.

" Good evening," said Hereda.

" Good evening," said the carabinero.

" Good evening," said the others.

Hereda came forward close to the gate. " We were wondering if we could go in."

" It's shut for the night."

" You couldn't let us in, I suppose ? "

" I'm here to stop you." The man smiled weakly and looked at his rifle.

" You wouldn't stop us, would you ? " said Hereda.

" It wouldn't hurt anyone if we went in."

The man was afraid, he couldn't see exactly how many of them there were. " No one's allowed in at this time of night," he said, with an ingratiating smirk.

Fuentes and Perez stepped forward. " Poor thing! Poor thing! " murmured Fuentes, nudging Perez.

" Poor who ? " said Perez.

" Poor girl, after coming all the way from England."

" Yes, all the way from England," said Perez, movingly, " travelling day and night."

" Just to lay some flowers on her uncle's grave." Fuentes signalled to Maria to step forward. She did so, holding her flowers and trying to look tragic.

" It's her last chance," sighed Hereda, " she's leaving first thing to-morrow morning."

They shook their heads and looked at the ground.

" I suppose," said Perez confidentially to the carabinero, " you must be wondering why she couldn't come in the day time ? Well, her other relations won't let her. It's a tragic story."

" He was my favourite uncle." Maria turned a giggle into a noisy sigh. " Uncle Jaime."

Ignacio now moved forward and looked hard at the carabinero. " We all remember Jaime," he said. " We all loved him. He was a man in a thousand." He turned to the others. " Do you know I was with him when he died ?—He kept asking after you, Maria—and I couldn't tell him why you weren't there."

" That would have been terrible," said Fuentes.

" It's a tragic story," said Perez, " the saddest story I know."

" Yes. We all loved him—Jaime," said Hereda, reverently.

The carabinero obviously didn't know whether to believe them or not, and must have decided to humour them. " I'm sorry," he said, " but I'm not the only one here."

" What ? " said Perez.

" I don't see any others."

" Well, they're in that house there." He pointed to a small house on the other side of the road. " If I were to open that gate for you they'd hear."

" We can climb over."

" If you were to climb over, the Guardia Civil down there might see you and fire. If they missed you and you got over, you'd find three dogs in there which would tear you to pieces."

They didn't know whether to believe him or not. Perhaps their imagination had fired his.

"We'd hear the dogs barking," said Hereda, suspiciously.

"Oh no, only when you try getting over," said the carabinero.

They walked away to consult each other about the situation. They spoke in a whisper.

"It's no good," said Perez, in despair. "There may not be dogs, but I know the guardia lives down there."

"I don't believe in the dogs," said Fuentes. "One, two or four I could have believed, but three is just the mystic number which would occur to a lying carabinero."

"That man's obviously been picked for the job for his teeth," said Hereda.

"I think they're beautiful," said Ignacio, "gold teeth that look silver in the moonlight."

Hereda sang softly into Maria's ear, "Your shining pearls are dim beside the gleaming silver jewels of death below the tall cypresses."

They came back to the gate. "Do you remember the days of Primo de Rivera?" said Hereda conversationally to the carabinero.

"Yes, Señor."

"Did you like them?"

Not knowing the political opinions of his questioner and sensing that whatever they were they were likely to be strong, the man hedged. "Well, I was in the provinces. It didn't make much difference there."

"This is his anniversary. He was buried here. Interesting —eh?"

There was something menacing in Hereda's voice. Afraid of an anti-climax, they were all bad tempered.

"Yes, it's interesting," said the man with another smirk.

"Do you know whereabouts his grave is?"

"No, I don't know that."

"You don't know which end or anything?"

"Probably down there," said the man, pointing to the other end of the cemetery, most likely because he wanted to get rid of them.

" Why do you think he's down there ? "

" Well," he floundered, " I don't know, but I think perhaps."

" I wonder where Uncle Jaime is ? " said Maria. There was a hush after his name.

The carabinero shook his head sadly, and they walked slowly away, along the white wall to the other end of the cemetery.

" A man of very little feeling," said Perez, loudly, so that the carabinero could hear.

" Living with death hardens one, makes one cynical," said Hereda.

They looked carefully along the bottom of the wall to see if there was anything on which they could stand in order to see over the top. They found a small grassy mound. Fuentes climbed on to it but couldn't see over the wall. " It's the best we can do," he said. He climbed down and Perez got up.

" Silence," he said to the others. He faced the wall, looked up at the sky and cleared his throat. " Primo de Rivera, former dictator of Spain, upholder of the monarchy! The monarchy has gone. The reactionaries have failed. We have a Popular Front Government! " He paused, then climbed down and turned to the others. " Those facts ought to be enough for him."

" We must rub it in," said Fuentes, and climbed up. " Primo de Rivera! Now we are free to say what we could not say in your time. Long live Republican Spain! Long live liberty! Long live the Revolution! "

" Olé! " said the others.

" That's enough," said Hereda, " I always had a weakness for him. Give him this from me." He took his rose out of his buttonhole and handed it to Fuentes. Fuentes threw it over the wall.

" I want to give him one, too," said Maria, " for a Miss Pearson." She picked a rose from her bunches and handed it to Fuentes. " And another—for Alonso."

15

The following days seemed to pass slowly. Maria spent most of her time in the library. Hard work now would mean more free time when Alonso came back. She smoked more, ate a great deal of milk chocolate. Every day at tea time she went to a pastry shop, ate rich cakes and drank thick chocolate and sugared water.

She met Rafael and his friends a few times in Baviera, but declined his offer to go to a film.

Ignacio phoned while she was out but left no message. By chance she ran into him as she was about to change trams on her return from the library. He dragged her off for a walk round the Retiro.

He was in an extraordinary mood and made her circle round the trees with him until she felt dizzy, then leaving her on a bench, he went over and spoke to some children. She couldn't hear what he said, but he made them scream with laughter.

" It was an experiment," he said.

" For what ? "

" Ha ha." He was unshaven and wore a white flower in his buttonhole. Before she went home he reminded her, " Tell Alonso to go to Paris. I'll get a studio for him."

" How can I ? "

" Oh, girls can make people do anything."

As they parted, he asked her to come and see him in Paris.

" All right."

" On your way back, when your train stops in Paris, phone me up and I'll come and meet you."

However, he forgot to give her address or phone number. That evening he left Madrid and she saw no more of him.

A letter came from Alonso, postponing the date of his return. She decided not to answer it. Her irritation with him was growing all the time. The reconciliation at their last meeting had been temporary and she regretted it. He must be amusing himself in San Sebastian and his talk about the portrait taking longer than he expected, because the sitter was ill for two days, was probably just a blind. It was probably untrue that he had gone there for a portrait at all. However, all this would perhaps never have come to a head if it had not been for the day of the General Strike.

The General Strike in Madrid lasted for one day only, but it was one of the best strikes ever organised. The decision was made the evening before, and in the morning the town, instead of waking up and moving, became more paralysed than during the night. There were no buses, trams, taxis or lorries. The metro was shut. Not one shop opened, not one café. Very few private cars ventured out, and those that did carried a red cross flag to show they belonged to the medical profession. No one left their house unless it was absolutely necessary.

Near lunch time some strikers came up to the Pension to ask the maids, the cook and the waiter to join them. They were going into every hotel and Pension, urging the staff to strike. A number of servants in private houses also joined the strikers.

Maria was confined to the Pension all day. There was no question of her going out. For some reason the central heating was not functioning, and it was the most bitterly cold day there had been yet in Madrid. The room was like an ice box. Fully dressed and wearing two coats and a pair of woollen gloves, she lay on the bed covered by a blanket, and even then she was frozen. She stayed there until lunch time reading coplas and St. John of the Cross. She felt as though she was the only person left in Madrid. There was no sound from the street, either of voices or of traffic.

At lunch time, everyone in the Pension was gloomy. The waiter and the cook were still there, but the maids had left. The proprietress was very angry and stood by the table of some young men whom Maria thought to be Fascists, complaining. Maria asked the waiter why he hadn't joined the strikers.

He shrugged his shoulders. " It's very difficult." He seemed to enjoy the strike all the same, and when he brought her in some fruit, said quietly, " There are lots of Marxists. Azana's a Marxist."

" Not exactly a Marxist."

" Yes, they say so."

Maria had not yet discovered that the term " Marxist "

could be applied to anyone who was not on the Right in Spain.

After lunch, she returned to her icy room, feeling a little better after some hot coffee. She was forced to get under the blanket again in half an hour. She read for some time and then felt so freezingly cold that she threw the book down and jumped up. This had the effect of making the only parts of her which had been warm as cold as the rest. She rang the bell and no one answered. She went to the office and spoke to the son of the house.

" I'm sorry," he said, " the boiler's out of order and we can't have it seen to on a day like this."

" Isn't there anything you could do to warm my room ? "

" I'm afraid not, Señorita."

Back in her room, colder than before and knowing that nothing could be done about it, she walked up and down and shed some angry tears. This did not last long. She realised the absurdity of such thoughts as, " I hope I catch cold and die, then these Pension people will be sorry! " and returned to bed. Sleep was impossible. It was worse than being alone on a desert island—there at least one would have something to look at— here was nothing but a great poster on the cinema opposite showing Freddie Bartholomew dressed as David Copperfield. There was no book in the room which she had not read before.

She turned out the pockets of the coats she was wearing and found three letters of Alonso, including his last one. She read them each several times, and then her fury began to vent itself on him. She felt that her cold and boredom of this day were somehow due to him, that he had never considered her for one moment, that there he was in San Sebastian, where there was probably no strike, and perhaps the sun was shining and in any case it would be warmer because of the sea, sitting in a café enjoying himself. What a gullible creature she had been to swallow his declarations of love and affection, though it was quite plain that if he loved her he would want an affair, and would certainly not go away for a week like this. And why did he like seeing her so much ? Vanity, of course. She had always thought him wonderful, he could see that and it flattered him. And why had she thought him so wonderful ? Because of Manolo's

talk, of course, before she had even met him.   But everyone
didn't think him wonderful.   Rafael and his friends thought of
him as a good sort.   Fuentes and Hereda looked on him as a
joke.   Ignacio thought him affected through and through.

She toyed with the idea of never seeing him again, but couldn't
face it.   She would see him, but she would be very careful.   She
certainly wouldn't fall in love with him.   And she would be sure
never to flatter him any more.

E

PART THREE

MADRID. TOLEDO. ST. JEAN DE LUZ.

EASTER 1936

1

ONE morning, Alonso rang up at half-past nine to say that he was in the café by the cinema. He had arrived early from San Sebastian that morning, had since been home, had a bath, shaved, eaten breakfast and was now longing to see Maria. He implored her to come and join him at once.

His arrival surprised her, because he had postponed his return twice. She had exactly a week left in Madrid. It was a Monday and she was leaving the following Monday.

When he saw her in the doorway of the café, he sprang up from his chair, hurried to meet her and gave her a loud kiss. " How I've looked forward to this! " He kissed her again.

" So have I," she said drily. She had a slight cold and that made her voice thick, nasal and distant.

" What's the matter ? " he asked after they sat down.

" Oh, nothing. I've got a cold."

" Poor thing. Aren't you glad to see me ? "

" Oh yes—very."

He ordered coffee and described to her his time in San Sebastian, the portrait, the sitter, her family, her tastes. Maria listened without comment.

" I've got a present for you." He produced a yellow-covered book from his pocket, " Swann's Way."

" Thank you very much." She took the book from him and turned over the first few pages.

She sniffed. " Go on telling me about San Sebastian."

He had not lived in his family's house, but in his aunt's. He described his aunt, uncle and cousins to her. He had seen Miss Pearson once, but she had not seen him.

When they had finished their coffee, they walked to another café. Alonso was talkative and affectionate, and made Maria wrap herself up in his scarf and wear his gloves.

In the next café they drank more coffee and he asked her what she had done in his absence.

" I worked a lot. I saw Ignacio twice and the others in Baviera.

" You did a lot."

" It wasn't interesting."

" Poor Marichu."

She suddenly turned on him. " Don't call me that."

" Why ? "

" Because I don't like it. Please don't."

" All right." He shrugged his shoulders.

They moved to the Negresco. Now Alonso was not so talkative, but subdued by Maria's outburst.

In the Negresco she kept sneezing and felt sorry for herself. Alonso laughed at her miserable appearance.

" You took a long time over the portrait," she said.

" Not as portraits go. Some people take years over them, three hundred sittings ! "

" Yes, but *they* take them seriously."

" It was a huge portrait. Life size, three-quarter length."

" I dare say you were lazy about it."

He laughed. " I have a lazy nature, you know."

" Then if you hadn't been lazy, you could have come back before. It's so silly of you to think you can make everything all right by bringing me books."

" Darling Marichu, I only brought you one book."

" It doesn't matter how many you brought me."

He laughed again. " If you feel like that, goodness knows what you're going to say when I tell you I've got another present for you."

" I like being given presents very much." She didn't ask what it was.

A walk was out of the question because her cold might get worse and it was damp out. He offered to take her in a taxi to the Prado, the Royal Palace, the exhibition of collages by Max Ernst, anywhere she liked. Taxis were cheap in Madrid and he said he had a lot of money now. Maria decided to stay in the café because she had not sat in cafés for some time now. Later they moved to La Granja.

She rather hoped she would see Hereda or one of his friends, but they were not there. Alonso told her they did not frequent the large cafés but went to bars and tascas.

"They go to Chicote, though," said Maria, "to see the Señoritos."

No one came to La Granja whom they knew, and they left before lunch time. They went early to a small, warm restaurant, the first people there. Alonso implored her not to be angry with him. "I've been making tremendous plans," he said. "I've got lots of money now and your last week will be marvellous. You can go anywhere you want, eat at any restaurant you fancy, go to theatres, cinemas every day—anything! But first of all we must go to Toledo. I've always wanted to take you there. We'll do it in great style. I'll borrow the family car and we'll drive there. We'll start out tomorrow after lunch, find a nice hotel, have a delicious supper, including partridge—partridges are a great speciality there—and then we'll walk about the town in the dark. The next day we'll see El Greco's house, the Cathedral, the Burial of the Conde de Orgaz—everything! Would you like that? Say you would."

"Yes, I would."

After lunch her eyes ached and her head was swimmy. "It may be a touch of 'flu," said Alonso, and persuaded her to go back to the Pension and lie down until the evening.

"You really want to go to Toledo?" he said as he left her.

"Yes, I do."

In the Pension she asked for a hot water bottle and was given a tin one. While she was undressing, the maid came in with a bundle of magazines and papers. "A gentleman brought these for you," she said, and put them on the table.

Maria looked through these and then dozed. At half-past six, Alonso phoned to enquire how she felt and said that they must not get her up.

At five to seven he phoned again to find out if she was well enough to meet him for a drink. This time she went to the phone.

" Did you send me the magazines ? "

" Yes."

" Thank you.   It was very nice of you."

" Are you better ? "

" Much better.   I'm all right now."

He told her to wrap herself up well, and said he would call for her in half an hour.

All through the evening he was fatherly and made a great fuss of her. When they saw Pepe in La Granja he went over and brought Pepe back for her.

" I want to congratulate you on your strike," said Maria to Pepe.

Alonso had told her to be sure and say " your."   " If it was as uncomfortable for the ruling classes as it was for me, it must have been a great success."

" Yes, it was very well organised."   Pepe smiled proudly as though he alone had done the whole thing.

" The best organised strike I've ever known. Are you going to have any more ? "

" I can't tell you that, but there will be more if we consider it necessary."

" Who's we ? " said Alonso.

Pepe ignored this.   " It is now possible to organise strikes in such a way that they really are effective. Nearly all categories of workers are ready to co-operate with us."

" But who are you ? " said Alonso, smiling.

" The working class movement."

" But why should the working class co-operate with the working class movement, if it's the working class movement ? Or are you, Pepe, the working class movement, and the working class simply what co-operates with you ? "

This annoyed Pepe.   " You know very well what I mean," he said, " *I* count for nothing."

" Oh no," said Alonso.   " Where would the revolution be without you ? Where would the working classes be without their working class movement ? "

Pepe left them very shortly after this, and Alonso continued to refer to him as the working class movement for the rest of the evening. Maria thought the joke a bit unfair, but she couldn't help laughing at it each time it came up.

They sat in La Granja drinking for a long time. Alonso elaborated the plans for Toledo. He decided when he would call for her and what they should take. " You must take coats, handkerchiefs," he said, because her eyes were watery, and she had to blow her nose all the time, " and scarves."

After dinner, Maria felt feverish, and they decided that she must take some aspirin and go to bed. Alonso bought her a bunch of roses and took her back to the Pension.

" Goodbye." He kissed her before she got out of the taxi. " And you'll see how nice it will be in Toledo."

2

The next day Maria felt worse. She was sick, dizzy and heavy, quite unable to get up. Alonso phoned in the morning, and when he heard how she was, sent her a message telling her not to get up until she felt better.

A little later he sent her some flowers, the second part of " Swann's Way " and a note:

" Darling Marichu,

We'll go to Toledo to-morrow instead. It doesn't matter when we start. I should like to see you. If your Pension doesn't mind gentlemen visiting you when you're in bed, let me know. I shall call to see how you are after lunch, and they could give me a note from you then. I love you."

Maria decided it would be better if he didn't come to see her, not because she minded very much what the people in the Pension thought, but because she was looking so wretchedly ugly, so she wrote to him:

" Darling Alonso,

Thank you for the flowers and the book. It was very nice of you to send them. Your note was nice, too. I think it would be better if you didn't come and see me. I hope we can go to Toledo to-morrow. If we can't, and I have to spend another day in bed, I shall be fed up. Why couldn't I have had my cold while you were away, instead of the moment you came back ? "

Unfortunately, the next day she was no better and the journey had to be postponed once more. She told the maid to phone the library and tell either the caretaker or Padre Moreno that she was unable to come because she was in bed (she hoped that might cover her absence until she returned from Toledo). Alonso sent more flowers and messages and phoned often. In the evening she felt better and went to the phone herself when he rang up. She assured him that she would be well enough to go the next day, and he said he would call for her in the car at half-past twelve.

The next morning, Thursday, she spent trying to make herself look less unattractive. She covered the red tip of her nose in powder and then so as not to look unevenly powdered, put a great deal of powder all over her face. The effect was not good, but the best that could be done. She packed a few things in her smallest suitcase, including " Swann's Way " and Saint John of the Cross. By the time Alonso called for her she was quite ready.

He was surprised by her appearance. " What on earth have you done to yourself ? You look like a little clown."

" I had to do something. It's not easy to look nice after a bad cold."

" I didn't say it didn't look nice. It looks very nice."

Downstairs the porter watched her curiously as he saw her put her case in the back of the car and drive off beside Alonso.

As they left the outskirts of Madrid, he told her to look in the back of the car, and turning round she saw on the back seat a thick, black cloak and a large black hat, which she had very unobservantly not noticed before lunch.

" I shall look very artistic for you," he said.

He drove slowly because he thought one missed everything if one drove fast.

There was a supply of English cigarettes in the car, and a red carnation which he had meant to give her earlier on to wear in her coat. He himself wore a red carnation in the button hole of his thick, brown, belted overcoat, and he looked very plump and affluent. His hair was greased and had a highly polished look. He had not been so sleek for a long time. He wore thick, fur-lined, leather gloves and smoked his cheroot in a holder. He kept his half-closed eyes on the road, giving Maria a constant view of his singularly flawless profile.

" You look so distinguished to-day," she said, " almost vulgar."

He laughed. " When you're as fat as I am, it's difficult not to look vulgar."

They drove in silence for some time. The arid countryside and the occasional stone buildings, garages and houses along the road were dramatic.

" I should like to go all over Castille," said Maria.

" Next year I'll take you."

He sang some songs, humming when he came to a part where he had forgotten the words.

After some time, they came to a small tower on the right-hand side of the road. They slowed down. The tower had a castellated top, slit windows from which hung some fossils. Looking closer, they saw more fossils, jaw bones and other parts of what might have been prehistoric animals half buried in the ground, seeming to grow there like flowers. Beside the tower was a small stone house, also medieval in appearance. The gate bore the title, Casa Darwin.

" Who lives there, I wonder ? " said Maria. " Perhaps a Superrealist." " An admirer of Darwin's."

They stopped the car and looked at the house for several minutes. The more they looked at it, the more they saw how well it bore inspection, how fantastic and thoroughly worked out it was in every detail. It was like a miniature, partly ruined and then restored castle, shown up by the fossils, the age of the bones contrasting with the newness of the stones of the buildings.

They drove on, deciding to ask people about it when they returned to Madrid. Alonso talked about Surrealists and Superrealists. The only think he liked about them was their humour, although apart from Ignacio, none of the ones he knew were a patch on the Marx Brothers.

" What about Hereda ? "

" He's no more a Surrealist than I am."

" Why did he pretend to me he was ? "

" Oh, he'll fall in with anything. Both he and Fuentes don't care what they do, they're always in a violent, vicious good humour and they might do or say anything."

" Do you like them ? "

" I admire them."

" They go in for a kind of magic," she said, " it can be rather attractive."

" It's easy, I could paint Surrealist pictures if I wanted to. I think I could write Surrealist verse, too."

" They think everyone could if they wanted to."

" I don't believe it. They're all as proud as peacocks."

" So are all painters and writers."

" They don't pretend not to be."

" Except you." What Ignacio had said of Alonso's painting was on her mind, and she kept thinking of it. " Do you think you'll get to Paris ? "

" I hope so."

" And paint, I mean—take a studio there ? "

" I don't know."

" You shouldn't leave it too late."

" How late would that be ? "

3

The sun's rays slanted through cracks in heavy purple clouds, dramatically lighting the red soil and tall trees in the countryside round the town. Toledo itself, walled round, rose in irregular terraces up to the peak of the Alcazar. Tired, cold, hungry, her head throbbing, as though in a dream, Maria found herself driving slowly through the archway into the town, the light changing abruptly and becoming much darker as the sun disappeared again behind the thick cloud.

The car had to be parked in the first square they reached, which was, in fact, the main square, because the streets were too narrow to take a car higher up. Small boys and young lads kept pestering them, offering their services as guides. Most of them had bare feet and seemed to do nothing but hang around the square all day waiting for tourists. Alonso knew how to deal with them and cursed at them angrily.

Hot coffee and cakes in a warm, comfortable café revived them both, and they felt quite elated as they searched for a hotel which Alonso knew.

The alleys, for the streets were really no more than that, ran between old, plain-fronted houses, and were so narrow that no perspective could be seen, and to be there was like being at the bottom of a long well, conscious only of the thin strip of sky above. The combined smells of Spanish tobacco, coarse olive oil and garlic pervaded everything.

" It's very sombre," said Maria.

No life seemed to be going on behind the dark, often barred windows. Tiny *cul de sacs* ending in the front of a house with a grilled door, tight-shut, turned off the streets at intervals.

A few people were about. In the shadowed light their faces seemed to her more markedly Castillian (her idea of Castillian) than the faces of the Madrilenos. The cheek bones were higher and more prominent, the nostrils more strongly curved, the skin harder and browner, and the expression more austere. She watched them attentively and they looked hard at her, her light skin and hair being very removed from them. Although they must be used to tourists of all kinds, as the collection of mispronounced, foreign words hurled at Maria and Alonso by the small, would-be guides had shown, there were few at this time and they were still curious about them.

" It's almost their only source of income," said Alonso.

After a long walk, they found the hotel, and seeing that Maria looked pale, tired and cold, Alonso left her in a warm café while he went to arrange for rooms.

When he joined her, some time later, he stayed with her for five minutes and then left her again, this time for much longer, while he took the luggage from the car to the hotel and put the car in a garage for the night.

The café was dark and deserted. The only other person there besides Maria was a thin girl behind the counter who had the face of a bad-tempered, smouldering Madonna. Through the narrow window one could see part of the back of a house, and through the gap between the slightly opened door and its frame, a small stretch of rough pavement and a thin strip of grey wall.

By the time Alonso returned, Maria was despondent, huddled over her empty cup, watching the crystals of sugar left in the bottom, undissolved by the tepid coffee. " Is all Toledo like this ? "

He had brought his cloak over his arm. " This is for you to wear. You won't be so cold." He reassured her and said she would like Toledo better soon. " You mustn't be worried because you don't like a miserable little café."

" I liked it from the outside—Toledo, I mean. I liked the way it sloped up to the Alcazar, the way the roofs were like a series of shelves. I didn't realise everything was so close together. I feel shut in."

They left the café and went back to the square near the entrance to the town, Alonso humouring Maria's desire for an open space. She wore the cloak which reached almost to her ankles and made the Toledanos stare at her even more than before. Its weight and the silk lining made the cloak slide on her shoulders as she walked as though a strange hand kept touching her lightly.

They found a chemist and she took some aspirin. After a drink in a café, which looked on to the square, she felt better.

They went for another walk, up hill, away from the square, through the maze of dark alleys. As the daylight went, the shadows on the walls spread more darkly and they met fewer people. Overhead, the slender strips of sky were a thick, dark, rosy grey.

Unexpectedly, they found the end of a long alley to be a ledge, half way up the slope, projecting slightly over some houses in the lower part of the town. Here, where it was more open, one could see a wide extent of sky and it was not so dark. Colour was still visible, though even the colours which were bright in the daytime, the green of the trees and the small patch of grass by the river which ran below them, and the red of the earth, now appeared to be powdered with dark grey dust.

They leant over the parapet holding hands and looked down on to the river. The light went quickly, and it was soon impossible to distinguish colour any more. The air was still and chilly. The houses below them were dark oblongs with no light coming from any part.

Alonso released Maria's hand and pulled her arm. " It's too cold here. We must have some partridge and some nice red wine."

As they walked back towards the square, she became more talkative. " Why are there so few windows lit ? Why is everyone so gloomy ? Why are the houses so close together ? "

In a quiet, even voice, he answered her questions. " I think you imagine there are fewer windows lit than there actually are. You will see more windows lit farther down. I don't think everyone looks gloomy but perhaps that's because I'm more used to that expression. If you spend some time there you would see that people don't really look gloomy. Perhaps something harsh in their features and voices makes you think they're gloomy because it makes *you* feel gloomy. The houses are close together in order to protect them from the sun. In the summer the heat is terrible. If they weren't protected like that, the Toledanos would shrivel up."

She laughed and thanked him. " Am I being bad company ? "

" Of course not." He kissed the top of her head.

Near the square there were well-lit shops and a cinema. The

square itself was gay with its rows of parked cars and groups of soldiers who walked up and down eyeing girls and whistling. Maria cheered up.

" We'll have a nice drink before we eat," said Alonso.

While they drank, she questioned him further about Toledo, especially about his reactions to the town. He told her they varied every time he came. It was very different in different weather and at different times of the day. In the morning it was not at all mysterious, but animated and noisy, in fact, she was bound to be woken up much too early the next morning by the noises of the street. Then the houses looked gay and cosy, so close together, and the aspect of the faces, sombre in the late afternoon and evening, proved to be passionate and lively.

" But could you live here ? " she asked.

" I don't know. Not altogether perhaps, but for quite a long time."

" I don't think I could."

By the time they had dinner it was late. Maria's eyes ached and there was a buzzing in her ears. Before dinner she took more aspirin.

He did not attempt to liven her up until the partridge and wine came to help him. Then he made her take off her cloak so that she should not feel cold in the street afterwards, and patted her arm with one hand while he held his glass in the other. They drank to Toledo.

She soon forgot Toledo. The interior of the restaurant, well lit, warm, full of dark rich colours, might have been anywhere. He urged her to drink a lot of wine. " It'll warm you up."

She grumbled once more about the climate of Spain and the houses being so close together, and then gave herself up to a happier mood. By the time they were half way through the partridge, she was laughing immoderately at Alonso's imitation of her grumbling.

The partridge was rich and delicious. Alonso ate quickly, carrying huge forkfuls to his mouth. He spoke with his mouth full.

" After dinner, we'll go back to the hotel and you can go straight to bed." He smiled.

" It must be quite late."

" Yes."

" But not late enough to go to bed."

" Of course it is if you want to."

" Did the hotel find it peculiar that you should be staying there with a young woman ? Or perhaps they didn't ask you any questions. Didn't you have to sign anything ? "

" Oh, to avoid difficulties, I said you were my wife."

" But didn't they think it odd you should want separate rooms."

" No, they're adjoining rooms."

After coffee, they walked slowly back to the hotel. The rooms were small, clean and bare, with wooden floors and white-washed walls without ornament. The electric bulbs hanging from the centre of the room, under the plainest of shades, cast a pool of light below them, leaving the corners of the rooms in obscurity. She chose the smaller room and he picked up her case which had been lying beside his in the larger room and placed it on her bed, sitting beside it. She began to unpack, and he laughed when he saw " Swann's Way " and St. John of the Cross.

" Why did you bring them ? "

" I always like to bring books, even if I know I shan't read them."

He began to read " Swann's Way," while she finished un-packing. This annoyed her. " Please go away. I want to undress."

" All right." He took the book with him.

When she had finished undressing, she shouted through the door and got into bed. He came in, sat on the bed and looked at her. " You look very flushed, Marichu. Do you feel all right ? "

" I don't know, I may have a bit of a temperature."

" It's sad for you to make an excursion when you're not well, isn't it ? "

" Oh, it doesn't matter."

He picked up St. John of the Cross, which was lying on the table by the bed.

" Oh, don't start reading now," Maria snapped. " If you want to read, go and read in your own room."

" I won't read." He put the book down again.

" Oh, do if you want to.   Don't let me stop you."

" I don't want to."

" You must or you wouldn't have picked up the book."

" I didn't want to."

" Why did you pick up the book, then ? "

" I can't think."

" You try to humiliate me in every possible way."

" I don't."

" Yes you do."

" I don't mean to. I mean to make you happy. You make me happy."

" I don't mean to."

" Then it's unfortunate for both of us."

She laughed. " Alonso, do you love me ? "

" You must know I do."

" How can I know you do ? "

" I see you every day. When I go away I miss you and write to you. What else do I do now ? Let me think. Well—I give you presents, though you don't seem very pleased with them."

" How much do you love me ? "

" Very much."

" More than anyone else ? "

" I don't love anyone else."

" Have you ever loved anyone else ? "

" Not like this."   He laughed and patted her hand.

She took her hand away. " Oh, don't be so patronising. Anyone would think I was a child or a half-wit, the way you talk to me."

" They wouldn't. They'd think I loved you very much and you were always angry with me."

" Oh well, never mind." She went on, " Alonso, how often do you have prostitutes ? "

He smiled.   " Well, it varies, you know."

" Do you like them ? "

" I don't know."

" Do you ever have the same one twice ? "

" I have done."

" Do you talk to them ? "

" Yes."

" What do you talk to them about ? "

" It varies."

" Have you had any lately ? "

" Yes."

" In San Sebastian ? "

" Yes."

" You never told me about it."

" Well — "

" Well what ? "

" I thought you'd take it for granted."

" I suppose I do, really." After a pause, she continued: " I don't attract you. You might be honest and tell me I don't. It's silly to pretend you love me."

" I do love you."

" In such a peculiar way. You're not in love with me, are you ? "

" I think I am."

" If you were, you'd be attracted by me in every way."

" I am attracted by you in every way."

" That's not true."

He put the sheets round her neck. " You mustn't be cold. I'll ask for a hot water bottle. Perhaps you should take more aspirin. Would you like a bottle ? "

" Yes, please."

There was no bell in her room so he went into his. She heard him ask the maid for a bottle. He always talked to maids and waiters in a benevolent, good-humoured way. When he came back to her room, she said, " You're very much a rentier. You're bourgeois."

" Why ? "

" The way you talk to maids and have prostitutes and everything."

" I don't see the connection."

" Well, I do."

" I trust you, I'm sure it's there."

" Oh, do stop being patronising." She sighed. " I suppose the bottle will be a tin one."

He laughed. " Never mind." He teased her, saying, that when it came to foreign hot water bottles and trains she was very British and insular.

She interrupted him. She'd not been listening. " Anyhow, I'm probably not attracted by you in every way, either."

" I know you're not."

There was a knock on his door. He left her and returned with a large tin bottle. " It's hot. I must put something round it." He went back to his room and came back having put his scarf round the bottle. He handed it to her.

" Thank you," she said, " I suppose you want to go to bed."

" I'm not in a hurry."

They were silent for some time. Maria sighed. " I think you'd better go."

He shrugged his shoulders. " All right." He kissed her cheek. " You won't have more aspirin ? "

" No thank you."

" Shall I turn off the light ? "

" Yes, please."

He kissed her again, turned out the light and went to his room, shutting the door behind him.

Some time later he looked in. " Good night, Marichu darling. I hope you feel better in the morning."

She didn't answer. He stayed in the doorway a moment, then moved slowly into his room and shut the door quietly.

4

Maria woke up feeling she was being watched, and when she looked at the door she saw Alonso standing there smiling at her. " I came to see if you were awake," he said.   " How are you ? "

" You woke me up.   I wasn't awake."

" I'm sorry."

" Oh, it doesn't matter."

" Shall I order breakfast ? "

" Yes, if you like." She turned over and looked at the wall.

" What's the matter ? "

" Oh, nothing! "

He left the room. She would have liked to go to sleep again, but found it was impossible. She got up, put on a dressing gown and went to Alonso's room. He was lying on the bed, giggling.

" Why are you laughing ? "

" I was thinking of a story in Proust, about the Guermantes. They were asked to a party, you see, and . . ."

" Oh, don't tell me now."

" Why not ? "

" I don't feel like funny stories."

" All right."

" I think it's extremely affected to lie on your bed and laugh at a story in Proust. It must be the kind of thing you see yourself doing.   The kind of thing you try and live up to."

" What *do* you mean ? "

" It's very unconvincing."   She went over to the window. " Did you ring for breakfast ? "

" Yes."

" Well, I hope it arrives soon."

" I don't think it will be long now." He sat up. " Dearest Marichu, shall I go on with the story ? I'm sure you'd like it."

" I shouldn't like it. If you go on with it, I'll . . ."   She stopped.

" You'll what ? "

" I don't know what I'll do."

He lay down again and began to laugh quietly.

" Oh, for goodness sake stop laughing! " Maria turned round and looked at him. He was unshaven, puffy and very sallow in his purplish red dressing gown, comfortable and smug, like an Oriental rake. " How you can go on being so affected all the time, I don't know."

" But my darling, how am I being affected ? "

" Oh well, look at you, look at your expression, and I'm not your darling! "

" You are my darling."

" I'm not. I don't want to be."

" Yes, but I decide whether you're my darling or not, not you. What you mean is that I'm not *your* darling."

" No, you're not, far from it."

" But what have I done ? " He looked at her with a helpless smile.

" Oh, you're so affected! "

" Come and sit here." He patted the bed beside him.

" No. I want to look out of the window." She turned her back to him and looked down on to the cobble stones below. It seemed to be a fine morning, the strip of sky above was an even, solid blue.

The maid arrived with breakfast, said good morning to them cheerfully, and placed the tray on the bed. " Will you want anything else ? " she asked.

" No thank you," said Alonso.

When she had gone, he began to pour out. " How do you like your coffee ? " he asked Maria.

" Very white."

" Good, I like mine almost black."

" How interesting! "

" I shall soon think seriously that you don't like me," he said, sadly.

Maria left the window and came over to her coffee. She sat on the extreme edge of the bed and looked down at the floor. " I do like you," she said, relenting, " but I get so irritable in the morning."

" Well, I hope you like me." He touched her hand.

" Yes, I do." She drew her hand away, and then to cover up the gesture began to butter a roll.

While he munched his roll he looked at her fixedly. " Here I am, in Toledo with you," he said when he had finished chewing.

" Yes, here you are."

" Isn't that delicious ? "

She shrugged her shoulders.   " I suppose so."

" Aren't you glad to be here ? "

" Oh yes. Toledo's a very interesting place and I want to see the El Grecos."

" You shall see them this morning." He began to plan their morning. He always seemed to get excited when he spoke of what they would do together. He described which El Grecos they would see, the ones of the Apostles in El Greco's house, though, of course, they weren't really by him, and last of all the Conde de Orgaz. " But you're not at all excited," he protested after this. " You're not listening. You're not interested."

" Yes I am."

" Shall we go back to Madrid this evening or to-morrow morning ? "

" Whenever you like."

" Don't you mind which ? "

" Oh, we'll see how things turn out."

As soon as she had finished her breakfast, Maria got up from the bed and went towards the door of her room.

" Where are you going ? "

" To dress."

" Please don't go yet. Stay and talk to me while I shave."

" All right." She moved mechanically back to the bed.

" Don't you want to ? "

" I don't mind."   Her headache was better and the cold seemed to be clearing up, but it had left her feeling light-headed and despondent.

He kissed her hand, stroked it and jumped up. Standing up, he stretched himself with a long sigh and then went over to the wash basin and turned on the hot tap. When he had wet his chin, he turned round and looked at her. " Talk to me."

" I don't feel like talking."

When he had covered his chin with lather, he asked her, " Don't you think I should look rather distinguished with a white beard ? "

" You look distinguished already."

The wash basin was just by the window, and he stopped looking into the mirror and turned his attention to the street. " I don't know why I wanted you to see Toledo so much, why it should have been Toledo . . . I know, it was because of when we walked down the Calle del Angel when I hardly knew you and you said so sadly that you'd only been to Guipuzcoa and Navarre. All the time I'm picking up threads of that time. Supposing I'd said then, ' Very well, you *shall* see Toledo, you shall see it with me.' That would have been the thing to do. Probably you've secretly wanted me to do things like that and you're disappointed, because you are disappointed, aren't you ? "

She didn't answer, and he turned from the window and looked at her. " You obviously are. But you must give me some credit. Although I didn't say that at the time, here you are in Toledo with me. Given time, I shall see to it that we do everything. And we are in Toledo, we are." He rushed over to her and kissed her.

" You've put lather all over my cheek."

" It won't hurt."

" I know, but . . ."

He kissed her on the other cheek. " That's made it symmetrical." He took both her hands. " Darling Marichu, I love you, love you."

He kissed her heartily on both cheeks. " I dote on you." He went back to the wash basin and continued shaving.

" Why did you want adjoining rooms ? " said Maria.

" So that I could talk to you."

" Oh."

" Didn't you want adjoining rooms ? "

" I think it's odd to go away with people and have adjoining rooms just to be able to talk to them. You could talk to them in cafés."

" You could—but it's nice to talk to them in a great many different places." After that he was silent while he used his razor. He cut himself twice, splashed some water on to the two small wounds and came over to her. " Now I look better."

He began to hum a fragment of a tune over and over again, the first few bars of César Franck's violin and piano sonata. He looked at her meltingly. "I should like to spend a morning lying on my bed, holding your hand, describing to you in detail the exact nature of my feelings for you."

"I think I know them."

"No you don't."

"What are they, then ? Why do you like me ?"

"I don't know why I like you, I know how I like you."

"You like me because you know how you like me. You can see yourself with me. It fits in nicely with the rest of your affectations."

He went on humming. He lay down and looked up at her. The brown of his eyes and the yellow of his skin were warm against the white of the pillow.

"This time next week, where will you be ?"

"In England, I suppose, unless the boat capsizes. Those Channel boats are rotten."

"It must be quite late. Perhaps it would be nice to have a drink ?"

She jumped up and strode to the window. She looked out, seeing nothing .She turned round, hardly trusting herself to speak. "Drink! First Proust and then drink! Can't you ever be natural ?"

He got up, came over to her, put his arm round her shoulders. "I was saying what came into my head. I felt so natural and at ease with you."

"Oh, did you ?" She lifted his arm from her shoulder and placed it by his side. She turned round and looked at him with cold fury. "Alonso!" She spoke slowly and firmly. "You're nothing but a drunken poseur. Would you say you were a drunken poseur ?"

He stared at her for some time without answering, then he said, with an uneasy smile, "What ?"

"A DRUNKEN POSEUR!" She shouted it at him.

He continued to stare at her, uncertainly now, then giving up trying to get past her angry coldness, half shut his eyes. "I don't know. Perhaps it is a good description of me . . . Is it yours ? What does it mean ? "

" Yes, it is mine. You know perfectly well what it means. I'll explain it to you if you like."

He shrugged his shoulders. " All right."

" You're a man who has no real feelings at all. You've suppressed them all and now you manufacture them with the aid of drink." She paused, saw his expression composed except for a faint bewildered smile. Forgetting how the shape of his features gave him a permanent air of composure, which he was often far from feeling, she felt insulted by the slightness of his reaction. " You're really a failure, a most miserable failure and it's useless for you to try and buoy yourself up with drink—and Proust—I think if you ever mention Proust to me again I shall scream. I can't . . ."

" Proust," he said, smiling.

She didn't scream. She looked at him silently.

" Proust," he repeated, clearly and slowly, and then after a long pause, " I wanted to hear you scream."

" I didn't mean scream like that . . ."

" How did you mean it ? Did you scream in the way you meant it ? "

She turned away from him, controlled a desire to hit him and rushed to her room, banging the door after her.

In her room she didn't know what to do. She walked about, looked out of the window, threw off her dressing gown, lay on her bed, got up, went over to the wash basin, turned on the tap, turned it off, put on her dressing gown and rushed back to Alonso's room.

He was lying on his bed looking at the window. When he saw her he smiled.

" Oh, I know you're laughing at me," she said, deliberately blind to the good humour and affection in his face.

" I'm not . . ."

" I may seem very silly to you. You never do anything like this do you ? You're much too smug and affected. It's very easy for you because you never feel anything except what you manufacture . . ."

" Marichu, dearest Marichu . . ."

" Oh, don't call me that. Please don't ever call me that again. You don't feel anything, and I can tell you why you don't, because if you did—if you allowed yourself to be natural for a moment, you'd collapse. You *have* to prop yourself up all the time so that you don't have to admit you're a failure, a failure as a person, a failure as a painter, a failure as everything. You'd have to admit you were dissatisfied and unhappy instead of the smug, superior, detached spectator you think you are. Really, you're the most cowardly and dishonest person I've ever met."

Alonso did not reply. He was not looking at her but at the window. She waited for some time.

" Why don't you say something ? " she said at last.

He shrugged his shoulders and spoke very gently. " What would you like me to say ? "

" Oh, you always leave everything to me." She moved towards the window, automatically trying to put herself into the range of his vision. He looked away from the window, moving his head on the pillow until she could only see his profile. " You won't even answer. This kind of thing revolts you, I suppose. It doesn't fit into your idea of yourself. It isn't the kind of thing you can imagine yourself taking any part in. Your nice, delicious, fantastic relationship with me doesn't allow for this, does it ? You won't defend yourself because you shrink from admitting the existence of the things I say. Well, I don't care. I don't care how superior you are. I don't care how silly you think I am. I don't want to have to fall in with your ideas. Of course, we can't call them ideas because you won't admit to having anything so vulgar as an idea, your tastes! I'm not going to be made to behave as you want me to behave. I'm not —really I'm not."

She realised she couldn't get him to look at her, and this seemed even more humiliating. She went further than she wanted to. " If you were young, it wouldn't matter so much, but you're not. You may be young in age, but your character, your personality, is middle-aged and set. You'll never change. You'll go on being more and more what you are now. It's a terrible prospect, the same jokes, the same tastes, the same pose getting staler and staler, hardening into their mould. One can't go on with it." She pushed back some hair which had fallen over one eye. She was trembling a little. " Anyhow, I'm not dead like that. I may be silly, but I'd sooner be silly than be like you." She heard the beginning of shrillness in her voice and spoke lower and more quietly. " I think we'd better go back to Madrid as soon as we've seen the El Grecos—or before, if you like—and when we get to Madrid, I think the best thing would be to end the whole thing. There's no point in going on with it, is there ? "

He didn't answer.

" Is there ? " She waited.

" No. Not if you don't like me," he said.

" That's right. Blame it on to me. You know perfectly well it's not because I don't like you. It's because you're what you are, superior, affected and . . ."

" It seems to me it's the same thing as your not liking me."

" It's impossible to argue with you." She went back to her own room.

5

After an outburst, Maria always felt better, and as she dressed she became sorry for what she had said. She had got it off her chest at last, and now she wished she hadn't. " Still, I've often criticised him before, and he has me too, and we thought no more of it! " she thought, to reassure herself. She remembered how kind he had been to her, how this excursion had been made just to give her pleasure and she decided that she must make it up with him at all costs. The trouble was that, although her bad humour had dispersed itself, the post-flu depression had not.

When she was ready, she knocked timidly on his door, wondering what he would say to her, and went into his room. He was dressed and sitting by the window.

" Shall we go and see the El Grecos ? " she said, brightly.

" All right."

" Shall we do it in the order you said ? "

" If you like."

" We'll do our packing later, shall we ? "

He nodded. They went downstairs silently and out into the street. Alonso knew the way and led her first to the Cathedral. This building was a mixture of styles and impossible to see properly from the outside because on all sides it was surrounded by narrow alleys and looking up one could only see a small part of the wall at a time. Inside, there were various things he wanted to show her. He took her to them, not holding her arm, or looking at her, but telling her quietly where he wanted her to go and what he wanted her to look at. As they went out, he asked her if she would like any photographs or pictures to take away with her. She shook her head.

" Would you like a cup of coffee before we go any farther ? " he said.

" Yes please."

" I think the nicest café is in the square. You can get very good chocolate there. Would you like chocolate instead of coffee ? "

" Yes, I would." She looked at him worriedly. " I'm very sorry. I didn't mean anything I said. I hope you didn't believe me." She put her hand in his.

He took her hand, but did not press it or look at her. When they reached the café he ordered two cups of chocolate and made her sit near a radiator and keep warm. His consideration struck her more forcibly then it ever had before, and her eyes filled with tears.

" We needn't go back to Madrid until to-morrow, if you like," she said.

He smiled at her. " I think perhaps we might as well go back to-day."

" If you want to."

" One can see quite a lot in one day. If we were going to stay a week then we could see it more thoroughly, but two days is much the same as one."

" But we needn't go back to Madrid until quite late, need we?"
" No."
" Good. I think Toledo's wonderful, but I think I ought to
spend a long time here in order to enjoy it properly. Next time
I come to Madrid I shall spend a week in Toledo." The idea
of spending a week in Toledo without an Alonso to show her
round and talk to her was meaningless. " It will be nice to
spend a week in Toledo. I shall also go to the Escurial. It's
silly of me not to have seen it this time. I'd meant to see it.
Perhaps I shall see it from the train on my way back, although, of
course, one can never see very much from the train." She
wanted to hear Alonso's voice, so she went on, " Can one ? "
" No one can't see very much."
Their chocolate arrived, very hot and accompanied by biscuits
to dip into it.
She smiled at him brightly from time to time as she ate. " It's
nice dipping it into the chocolate, isn't it ? It's a nice sensation.
While you were away, I did this a lot, every afternoon I drank
chocolate," she added, with feeling, " because I missed you so
much."
He laughed.
She laughed uproariously, too. " Oh dear, how silly I am,
and how well you know how silly I am. It's absurd of me to
criticise you—not that I was criticising you this morning,
because, of course, criticism is something you mean and that
wasn't anything I meant, it was just an outburst, a silly, childish
outburst. You didn't take it seriously, did you ? You can't have
done, not knowing me as well you do."
Alonso gave her a slight smile, his eyes were not smiling, but
half shut, the thick, heavy lids above making the eyeballs appear
to have a light film over them. " Well, an outburst can be the
release of things which have been there some time. One can
tell when it's that, I think."
This frightened her. " Well, then you could tell it wasn't
that with me. I'd never thought any of that before."
" But you've said it before. Not quite so firmly as that, but
I have heard it before."
" Oh no. I've said you were lazy and we disagreed and so

on, and I still think you're lazy, not that it matters whether you're lazy or not. I like people to be lazy, I'm frightfully lazy myself, but I said much more than that this morning, and I didn't mean it. I can't even remember what I did say. That just shows." She could remember perfectly well. " Anyhow, whatever you are, I like you. This made everything sound much worse, so she added, " I love you."

" I don't think you'd like—or love," his emphasis and the slight pause after the word love made him sound ironical, " anyone whom you considered a failure."

" Well, that proves it. I do love you so obviously I can't consider you to be a failure, can I ? " She persisted, " Can I ? "

" I suppose not." He smiled at her. " But in a sense I am a failure. There are very good grounds for considering me to be a failure."

" None that count with me."

6

After the café they walked to El Greco's house hand in hand. Maria was far more impressed by this house than by the cathedral. She looked down the well in the garden for a long time, looking for the beginning of the elaborate network of under-ground passages which connected the well with the river, down which the Jews had escaped during persecutions. She also liked the pictures of the Apostles, and when Alonso explained to her why it was obvious they were by a pupil of El Greco's and not by the master himself, said she could have guessed that, and later admitted that she wouldn't have been able to tell. She liked the picture of Toledo and stood in front of it a long time, asking Alonso to explain to her why she should like it so much.

They walked through the house several times and then went back and looked down the well. The guide came over to them and explained at great length where the secret passages led and who had used them. Alonso pretended that he knew much more about it, he told the guide that he had spent the best part of his life researching into that well and he had proved conclusively that no Jew had ever used it, but only Moors. " It would take too long to go into how I arrived at this interesting conclusion," he ended. " But scholars like Señora del Arbol, the English scholar Miss Pearson, and the Irish scholar Miss Marichu, are in complete agreement with me. No doubt some scholar may appear in the future," he made a broad pompous gesture with his arm, " who will find flaws in my evidence, and I shall be grateful to him, for what I care about is truth, TRUTH, not my conclusions, but until he appears, until then, I must consider that I am right."

As they walked away he said he hoped that had upset the guide, and that in future he would tell people the well was never used by Jews.

It was now time for lunch and they found a nice, small, comfortable restaurant near the square. Alonso decided that the next time he came to Toledo, he would argue with all the guides, and make them believe that Velasquez painted the Apostles and Murillo painted the Burial of the Conde de Orgaz. He would think of a lot of things to confuse them, then perhaps they wouldn't be so anxious to come and pester him. He would be marked out as the man all guides must avoid. They spent a long time thinking of things which it would be interesting for guides to believe, and ended with a decision that the Surrealists and Superrealists would be best employed as guides in Toledo. They wouldn't take one to see the usual things at all, but would conduct one to some old poster in the square. There would be some point in that, because they would show things that otherwise one would not have noticed, whereas the guides did nothing but show you things which you would see much better without them.

They had left the Burial of the Conde de Orgaz for the afternoon, but did not feel like going to see it immediately after lunch.

" We'd better not leave it too late," said Alonso, " or the light will be too bad."

" Well, we'll go there soon."

" Let's go back to the hotel now and pack."

" That means we are going back to-night ? "

" Yes."

" You're still angry with me."

" I was never angry with you."   He laughed.

When they reached the hotel he told her to go on upstairs while he explained to the people that they were leaving, settled the bill and arranged to get the car out of the garage where it had been placed for the night.

She packed her things at once, there was very little to pack, and she had quite finished by the time he came up. " Shall I help you ? " she said.

" Please."

While she packed for him, he sat down by the window and looked out. She looked at him and then went over to him. She saw one tear trickle slowly down his cheek. Her own eyes watered. " Oh, Alonso! " She threw her arms around his neck and kissed him.

He went on looking out of the window and patted one of her hands as though he was trying to calm her.

" Darling Alonso, let's go to-morrow morning. It seems such a pity to go back to-day."

He shook his head. The tear trickled to his chin and then disappeared. There was no trace of another, but Maria could only see one side of his face. " Darling Alonso," she repeated, " if only you knew how much I loved you."

He turned round and smiled at her. " We'd better hurry up with the packing. We mustn't get to the Conde too late."

" All right." She kissed the top of his sleek head and hurried back to the packing. He assisted her by collecting his shaving things and threw them in on top. The black cloak was thrown over a chair. " Would you like to wear this ? " he said.

" No, you wear it. I wore it last night and I want to see you in it."

When the packing was finished and the case lying next to Maria's on the floor, he picked up the cloak and threw it over his shoulders. It suited him admirably, emphasising his height and bulk and showing up how well set his small head was on a long, thick neck. He went over to the mirror.

" You must have your hair absolutely smooth," said Maria.

He smoothed back his hair with the palm of his hand.

" You look wonderful," said Maria. " I had thought you looked Chinese, but after seeing a lot of El Greco's, I can see the Spanish part of your face, it's the nostrils and that tight, curly kind of mouth. Your profile doesn't suggest that your front face is so flat, it's much more Spanish than your front face, and from the side one can't see that your eyes slant. I like your face more than any other."

" Thank you." He smiled, " and your face . . ."

" Oh, my face is very ordinary. I daresay more people would think me pretty than would think you handsome, but you know what you think of my face. It's not in any way so distinguished as yours. Perhaps Toledo is a good setting for you, but I've never seen you look so Castillian. You must be Castillian. I can't believe you're Basque."

" Pure Basque."

" Weren't any of your ancestors Castillian ? "

" Probably, but none of them were Chinese."

" I shall be very proud to be seen out with you in that cloak. You must wear it in Madrid."

As she walked beside him in the street, Maria was absorbed in Alonso's appearance. He threw back one side of the cloak in order to be able to hold her hand easily. As he walked, the cloak swayed and from the side he was entirely her idea of the proud and melancholy Spaniard of Golden Age literature. She thought of his name. " Why are you Alonso and not Alfonso ? " she asked.

" It should be Alfonso, but the ' f ' got left out ? "

" When ? "

" I can't remember when."

" When you wore your cloak and black hat ? "

" Oh no, long before then. When I was so high." He bent down indicating that he must have been six inches from the ground at the time. This made her laugh.

When they reached the church, Alonso had to talk to a young priest and then to an old man before they were allowed to see the picture. At last they were led over to it, and the old man began to murmur an explanation.

" It's all right," said Alonso, " I know all about the picture. It's my special subject." He bent down and whispered loudly into the old man's ear, " We're art historians." After that they were left alone.

They looked at the picture for a long time. The light was not good, and it would have beeen wiser to see it in the morning. The dead nobleman, with his grave-faced, black-clad mourners, was overwhelmingly upsetting.

" Do you like it ? " asked Alonso.

" I don't know."

Afterwards she questioned him about the Conde, who he was, what he did, how he died, who were the mourners. " Sometimes I can't bear that side of Spain," she said. " It's all death and vanished splendour. I suppose it was all right if you believed in heaven, because then you went to new and more glorious splendours. One would have to be religious if one were a Spaniard or die of melancholia. The burial of the Conde is like Toledo. It's like you, especially in your cloak. It's like you when you spoke of Gongora."

7

Back in the comfortable café, where they had drunk chocolate in the morning, she urged Alonso to talk, plying him with questions and applauding everything he said. She longed for him to realise how much she liked being with him. " You are the only thing that matters in my life! " he had once said. Why hadn't that been good enough for her ? What else could he say ?

She had described the trip to the cemetery to him, and they

were back to Surrealism again. He explained why Ernst's
Semaine de Bonté was placed in the period it was. "That
style can end in birds' heads and fishes' tails. There's an animal
beneath the bustle, the pigeon bosom, the narrow trouser, the
fluffy side whisker, the moustaches."

"You could go in for that kind of thing if you wanted to."

"I prefer Popeye at 600 pesetas a week."

He seemed tired and pensive, looked blankly at her, and had
to be asked questions several times before he could take them
in. He cut short any attempt to refer to what she had said in the
morning, politely but firmly.

Suddenly he stood up. "I must go and get the car. I'll be
back soon."

It was raining. The sky was black and heavy and already the
café was lit.

He returned, rain dripping from the shoulders of his cloak
and the broad brim of his hat. To protect her as they walked, he
threw part of his cloak over her.

"Thank you," she said.

They entered the car, shut the doors. He took off his hat and
threw it on to the back seat, took the key out of his pocket,
inserted it, but did not switch on the engine.

She looked at him. He was staring at the switchboard,
motionless. She looked out of the window to see if anything
could be holding him up. She coughed.

His hand was on the key, ready to turn it. She waited for
what seemed ages. "Alonso, is there . . . ?"

He turned on the engine and they drove off, across the square
now deserted by the little boys. He switched on the screen
wiper and to the accompaniment of its steady moan they slowly
left Toledo, through the archway and out on to the open road.

8

There was no pause before she was put down at the door of the
Pension. " I must hurry home," said Alonso, " I haven't the
key of the garage, and I don't want to get there after the man's
gone."

" I'm glad we went to Toledo.   It was lovely."

" I'm glad you liked it."

He carried her suitcase to the lift.   " Goodbye," he said.

" Till to-morrow ? "

" Yes."

" When ? "

" I'll give you a ring sometime."   He left her.

She rang for the lift, turned round, saw him get into the car
and ran after him.   The door of the car was still open and she
put her head inside.   " I think I've upset you.   I didn't mean a
word I said.   Oh, Alonso . . ."

" It's all right, Maria.   Please don't be worried."

In her room she flung herself on the bed, expecting, perhaps
hoping, to burst into tears, but she remained dry-eyed and calm
with a very clear head, remembering everything with a sickening
clarity when she would have liked to blur it with a great wave of
emotion.   At last she opened her suitcase.   The first thing she
saw was " Swann's Way."   She picked it up and flung it savagely
on to the floor.   St. John of the Cross followed.

9

The following morning she was up by eight.   At nine she
phoned Alonso.   He was not up.   At half-past nine she phoned
again, found him still in bed and left an urgent message that he
should ring her.   At ten she phoned again and found he had
left the house.

At half-past ten she had to leave for the library. It was necessary for her to spend time there clearing up that day, because
the next day would be Sunday, and after that she would be
leaving Madrid.

Padre Moreno was at his desk. He rose and shook hands with
her.

" I haven't done much work this week," she said, " with this
wretched cold."

" You don't look at all well."

" I'm better now."

She began to sort out her notes. She looked up and saw
Padre Moreno watching her. " It's my last day in the library,"
she said, " I'm leaving early on Monday morning."

" So soon ? What a pity ! "

" I know. I don't want to leave Madrid."

He smiled and rubbed his hands. " You like Madrid ? "

" Yes. I should like to live here."

" Ah," he sighed, " It's not always possible to do what we
want to do."

" No, it isn't. I wish it were." She found it difficult not to
imitate him. She sighed and shook her head. " It's not always
possible to know what we want to do."

" That's very true."

By lunch time she noted with little satisfaction that she had
almost finished all the work she was supposed to do.

She returned after lunch in a taxi with an empty suitcase. A
further phone call to Alonso had found him still out.

The caretaker had heard from Padre Moreno that she was
leaving. His chubby, red face wrinkled as he said, " So we
shan't see you after to-day ? "

" No. Next year, though, when I come to Madrid again, I'll
come and see you. Perhaps I shall work here again."

" I hope so, Señorita."

" It's the nicest library I've ever worked in."

He smiled proudly, and looked at the marble staircase which
he kept beautifully.

Padre Moreno did not arrive until late in the afternoon, about
a quarter to six. He was very worried because the Trustees

were not there that day, and Maria would be unable to say goodbye to them in person. " They will be extremely sorry to have missed you."

" I'm very sorry to have missed them. I should have liked to tell them how nice it was for me here."

They had a long talk about Madrid and Spanish literature. When it came to the political situation in Madrid, Padre Moreno sighed. " There may be trouble. Who knows ? "

They neither of them knew anything about each other's politics beyond the fact that they had once agreed that Christ's teaching was not unlike Socialism.

" Well, I hope there isn't any trouble," said Maria.

When she put her notebooks in the case and put back the books she had taken from the library she felt very sad, and when it came to saying goodbye to Padre Moreno she couldn't smile. He went with her to the front door, forming a group with the caretaker and his wife. They stood there and watched her as she went down the street to look for a taxi and she turned and waved to them several times.

10

Before dinner she looked in at Baviera, saw Rafael and his friends, and asked if they'd seen Alonso.

" No," said Rafael, " but he'll turn up if you're expecting him."

" I'm not exactly expecting him."

" Well, stay and have a drink with us, then."

She did, and waited there for half an hour, hoping that Alonso might appear.

Disappointed, she went on to La Granja, Chicote, the Aquarium and any other likely café, making her way through crowded tables, hoping that every portly man she saw might be him. No luck. " He wants to pay me out," she thought, " or else his Spanish pride has decided him never to see me again." It seemed to her now that she loved him, that she would have been really in love with him if he hadn't always insisted that it could come to nothing.

No messages had been left for her at the Pension, no one had phoned at all. He must have been told she had phoned, and he obviously wanted to avoid her. There was nothing she could do about it.

By the next morning, after a miserable evening and an almost sleepless night, she was sure that she would never see him again unless she ran into him by accident. It was the first warm, sunny day there had been for a long time, and she spent the morning walking through the streets and the Retiro, looking in at all their old haunts.

When she returned to the Pension for lunch, they told her that a gentleman had phoned and would be ringing again after lunch. Her spirits rose. After lunch the call came through. It was Rafael. She could have murdered him when she heard his cheerful voice. What an insipid man!

" I hear you're going to leave us to-morrow," he said.

" Yes."

" We thought it would be nice to have a farewell drink. Antonio is very anxious for it. How about Baviera at seven ? "

" Who told you I was going ? "

" Alonso."

She wondered if he would be there, but knew it would look odd if she asked. She clutched at it as the only straw. " Yes, I'll come."

That evening, in Baviera, she found Rafael, Antonio and Jaime at a corner table. They hailed her as an old friend and plied her with drinks. Even Jaime was friendly. The table was large enough to hold two more, but she couldn't tell whether they expected anyone else or not.

" And I still haven't persuaded you to change your politics," said Antonio.

" You never will."

" Next year, perhaps."

"If you come to Madrid again next year," said Rafael, "we won't let Alonso monopolise you all the time. We'll show you round."

She had to find out. "By the way," she said, casually, "where is Alonso?"

"Oh, he'll be here any moment."

That was better. She became elated and had as many drinks as they pressed on her.

At last she saw him come in, large and slow, and make his way to the table. Her eyes were shining and her cheeks were burning. He greeted them all and sat down facing her. He looked tired and blank, but contributed a little to the pointless conversation which went on.

Now she wished the others would go. They looked settled there for the night. Alonso made no move.

Finally Rafael had a brain wave. "How about us all having a meal here as time is getting on?"

Alonso seemed about to agree.

"No," she said, "Alonso surely you know we must be going. We've got to meet those people."

He hesitated for a moment. "Of course, I had quite forgotten."

She shook hands all round, thanked them for the drinks, for their good wishes, and promised to look them up next year.

In the street she asked Alonso, "Are you going to have dinner with me?"

"Yes."

During dinner she asked, "Why didn't you phone me or anything?"

"I was busy."

"What a lie. You're never busy."

"I had to do a lot, including packing."

"Whatever for?"

"I'm leaving Madrid when you do. I'll go with you as far as St. Jean de Luz and then go back to San Sebastian."

"But why go all the way to Saint Jean de Luz?"

"To gamble."

She was distressed. "If it's on account of me that you've

decided that, please don't, I didn't mean to upset you. I know you've every cause to be fed up, but please don't gamble. It will make me feel so wretched."

"You needn't worry, Maria, I gambled long before I even knew you existed."

She went on trying to dissuade him, urged him now that he had some money not to throw it away, but to do something with it, go as far as Paris, take a studio for a year as he had so often suggested and take painting seriously. Ignacio would get him one, he was longing for him to go, he thought he could be a great painter if he would only work hard.

"Nonsense," said Alonso, "Ignacio is an idiot."

"He's very fond of you."

"I like him, too, but he's an idiot."

She begged him for her sake not to gamble, to keep the money until she came back to Spain, and then they would have a wonderful time together. Surely, if he loved her, he would rather do that, or didn't he love her any more?

He avoided answering this. "And why do you assume I'm bound to lose?"

"You lost all the Popeye money."

"That makes it all the more likely I'll win this time."

"Oh, you won't, I bet you won't."

It was obvious that the idea of gambling excited him. He told her of the times he had won, and how wonderful money was when you got it like that, it seemed more interesting than when you earned it, it gave you a sense of power when you spent it. "I tell you what. If I win, I'll go on to London with you. Would you like that?"

"Yes, but I hate leaving things to chance."

He laughed. "You don't seem very anxious for me to go to London with you?"

"But I know you won't win. And besides, I can't imagine you in London. There are no cafés. Everything shuts at eleven, and places that don't are expensive and dreary. You'd soon be bored."

"Well, I probably won't win and then I shan't go to London, so never mind."

11

Alonso arrived at the last moment and managed just in time to
see Maria waving to him, and scramble into the compartment
where she had reserved a place. The train was crowded. They
were travelling third, because Alonso wanted to keep as much
money as he could for roulette. Maria, arriving at the station
very early, had secured two corner seats, but the compartment
was so tightly packed that there was no comfort anywhere.

They went out into the corridor, had a bet of five pesetas on
which side of the train the Escurial would be, and Maria won.
After that, Alonso went back to the compartment, pulled out
his case from under the seat—there was no room for it on the
rack—and took out a Spanish translation of an American
detective novel.

" Are you going to read ? " said Maria.

" No, I'm going to eat it," he said, and put a corner of the
book into his mouth.

She laughed. " I hoped you were going to talk."

" I don't feel like talking. I always read on long distance
journeys."

" I never thought you were the type of person who read
detective novels." She leant over and whispered quietly,
because by this time the people near them were listening.

" You've revised your opinion of me so often," he said,
smiling, " it won't hurt you to do it again."

He read solidly until the bell rang for the first lunch. As
they walked to the dining car, he seized the opportunity of being
alone with her at the end of a corridor to give her a kiss.

" I wonder you don't like detective novels," he said over
lunch. " They're very cultural. The hero of this one quotes
from the classics and knows everything about music."

" They're all like that," said Maria.

He laughed. " He's the most unsympathetic man I've ever
come across."

" He must be."

" He's just the type of man you'd fall in love with."

" Then he must be like you."

" Oh no, Marichu. I'm not your type at all. It's too late to pretend that now."

Lunch consisted of a heavy potato omelette, veal, beans and fruit. After that they each drank two cups of black coffee and smoked. Maria tried one of the cheroots, but abandoned it after a few puffs.

On the way back, he kissed her again in the corridor. They were seen by a young couple on their way to the second lunch, who smiled at them with sympathy.

" If they knew how misplaced that smile is," said Alonso.

Maria noticed the signs of his bitterness and felt unable to do anything about it. She decided it must be exaggerated by the journey, she knew he hated long journeys. She encouraged him to return to his book, which he did, while she stayed in the corridor, smoking and looking out of the window.

After a time, she went back to her seat and read a newspaper. Alonso's eyes were shut, the detective novel lay open on his lap, he was in a huddled position owing to the lack of space. His white, tapering hands looked helpless and abandoned.

At tea time she tapped him gently. He smiled and told her he had not been to sleep at all.

Once more they went to the dining car. " Having meals is a relief on a journey," said Maria.

" Yes."

" I'd thought a journey with you would be nice," she complained.

" Mistaken again! " He smiled, " Poor Marichu! "

12

When they reached Saint Jean de Luz it was dark. They went to the hotel nearest to the station and left their luggage.

" *Not* adjoining rooms this time," said Alonso.

Maria suggested a cup of coffee and something to eat, but Alonso was uninterested. " You go and have one if you like, but I'm going straight to the Casino."

She thought it best to go with him, hoping she might be able to restrain him when the time came.

The large, brightly lit roulette room seemed strangely empty. Apart from the two croupiers, the only people at the table were an old, white-haired man with lifeless eyes at the far end, and a young man near the door. In the corner was the cashier who changed Alonso's pesetas into francs and then into counters.

For a few minutes they watched the game, the mere sight of it appearing to soothe Alonso. The old man won every round, the young man's pile of counters dwindled.

" Now pray for me and wish me luck," said Alonso, and started off with five-franc pieces. He was cautious, and for the first few rounds won on evens, then he lost what he had won. Betting on reds and evens, he remained more or less where he was for some time. He began to get impatient. The old man had made so much that he threw two hundred franc pieces to the croupiers. They thanked him.

" Why don't you follow his game ? " said Maria.

" It would be fatal," said Alonso, " that would be quite wrong. His luck would go at once."

The old man was playing on numbers in the third dozen. Alonso stubbornly kept to the first dozen. He had soon lost fifty francs. Again Maria urged him to move into the third dozen or go back to reds and evens. This annoyed him. He pushed over some counters. " If you want to try with these, you can, but don't keep on giving me advice."

" I don't want to play. I should only lose." She pushed the counters back.

The young man had lost everything. He smiled at the croupiers, shrugged his shoulders and went out. The old man's luck still held, with very rare setbacks. He was playing with very high stakes, still in the third dozen. His pile of counters was imposing.

Maria began to loathe the croupier's nasal superior voice as he repeated, " Au jeu " and " Rien ne va plus," and the disdainful way he removed Alonso's counters as though they were too small to be of any interest.

" I'll have to change some more money soon, "said Alonso.

" No, don't. I know you won't win to-day. Why don't you wait and paint another portrait and come to England with *that* money and add what you've got left to it ? "

He smiled at her. " It's not because I want to go to England. I like gambling."

" I could understand it if it were somewhere gay with lots of people, but here with one old man and those beastly croupiers, it's depressing. It wasn't even exciting when you won."

" You wait till I really start winning, and then you'll see."

Before he converted more money into counters, he handed her three hundred pesetas. " Keep that for the hotel."

" I'll pay for myself."

" Nonsense, if it hadn't been for me you wouldn't have had to spend the night in Saint Jean de Luz."

" All right."   She put the money in her purse.

He had lost a hundred and fifty francs. He was a little irritated, but otherwise composed. He came back with his counters, sat down beside Maria and put ten francs on the first dozen. She knew this was fatal. The old man was still winning and keeping to the third dozen. Looking at his wrinkled, white, lifeless face, Maria was sure it was fatal to go against him.

" I don't want to watch you," she said, at last. " Perhaps it would be better if I didn't watch you. You might win then. I know you won't as long as I'm here."

" All right."

She went out into the corridor and walked about. A window at the end gave out onto the sea. It was windy and the waves were high and crested. They broke with a long, explosive sound, then drew back hissing to form once more. A cloakroom attendant with a sallow skin and tired eyes smiled at her. She felt grateful for this and returned the smile. She found some cigarettes in her pocket, the remains of a packet of Lucky Strikes Alonso had bought her while he felt rich. She lit one, went over to the window and looked at the sea. After about ten minutes she went to the ladies' cloakroom, combed her hair and talked to the attendant, who told her that it was a very bad season. It was so cold and rainy that there were no tourists this year. Even during Easter week, when people had holidays, the Casino had been practically empty every night.

"What about the people there to-night?" said Maria. "There's only one now."

"Oh, he lives here. He's here all the time."

"Does he always win?"

"I don't know." She shrugged her shoulders. "Probably not."

Maria went back to the corridor and watched the door of the roulette room. She could hear nothing. She opened the door and looked in. There was a tall pile of counters in front of Alonso. He didn't see or hear her. She shut the door. He must be winning. It was a good idea to have left him.

She went out into the street, to a café across the road, and ordered some hot coffee. She was hungry now, but did not want to eat until Alonso had finished, and they could have a meal together. There were only four other people in the café, sitting together, talking and gesticulating. After Spain, French gestures and voices seemed curiously artificial.

When she returned to the Casino, she found Alonso in the corridor. "I looked for you everywhere," he said. "Where did you go?"

"I had a cup of coffee."

"I thought you disapproved of gambling so much that you'd left me." He kissed her.

"Did you win?"

"For a bit." He smiled.

"I looked in and saw a huge pile in front of you."

"That was because I'd just changed all my money."

"Oh."

"I haven't any left now."

She was silent.

" Could you give me back a hundred pesetas ? "

" Oh, Alonso."

He patted her arm. " Don't look so miserable. What's a hundred pesetas ? I may make a thousand."

" You won't." Automatically, she opened her bag and gave him a hundred peseta note. He took it. " Come with me."

" No."

" But it must be so boring for you out here."

" It's worse in there."

He laughed, patted her shoulder. " I won't be long. As soon as I've doubled what I lost, I'll leave." He left her and went back to the room.

He didn't win. When he joined her he told her that at one moment he had got back three hundred francs, but those had slowly gone. He was cheerful. " I've still got two hundred pesetas. We'll have a nice meal. I'm afraid you'll have to pay for your hotel."

" I don't mind that."

" Cheer up, Marichu. Don't be so depressed. Next time I come, I shall win a million francs."

They went to a large, empty restaurant and had a delicious meal, which turned out to be fantastically expensive. Alonso insisted on paying.

" But you must leave yourself enough to get home with," said Maria.

" I shall have just enough to pay the hotel and get home."

" I think it's sad when people lose all their money."

" I'm not sad, so I don't see why you should be."

After dinner they walked back to the hotel. " So, I won't be going to England with Marichu after all."

" I never thought you would."

" You didn't want me to."

" I knew you wouldn't."

13

Maria woke early. It was bitterly cold and pouring with rain. It must have been raining for a long time, for outside the window wet surfaces shone, rivers of muddy rain rushed along the gutters overflowing onto the pavements. On the linoleum beneath the open window was a pool. There was a constant roar from the sea and the sigh and patter of rain.

She dressed and went along the passage to Alonso's room. There was no time to lose. Her train went in the morning and she must make it up with him before they parted. The night before he had seemed soothed and exalted by the gambling. Even though he had lost, it had been cathartic and satisfied him. " I like to leave everything to chance," he had said almost contentedly, and all she could think of was, " I am the master of my fate, the captain of my soul."

He was asleep and she hesitated before waking him.

" Good morning," she said, timidly.

He opened his eyes and stared at her.

" Good morning," she repeated.

" Good morning, Maria." His voice was thick and petulant, and he shut his eyes again.

" I know it's early to wake you, but I wanted to talk to you."

" You're indefatigable."

" Well, I don't want to leave you feeling like this, and there isn't much time."

" For goodness sake give me time to wake up."

" Shall I open the shutters."

" Please leave me. I shall get up soon and we can have breakfast."

She hung about uncertainly. He turned over and buried his face in the pillow. She left him and went back to her room, packed, went downstairs and found out how much the bill would come to (it was important to know this), gave notice and checked the time of the train.

They breakfasted in his room. He was dressed. She kept asking him what he was thinking. She always liked everything to be clear and to have it quite taped. She suggested what his state of mind might be, but all he would answer was " Perhaps."

" But Alonso, I love you. I must know whether you still feel anything about me. I don't mind it's not being an affair or marriage, or anything—you were probably quite right about that—but I do want you to feel as you felt before Toledo, and then when I come back to Spain we can go on as before—we were so happy together."

" You didn't seem very happy."

" Well, I was. I realise it now."

" Maria, all you had to do was to enjoy yourself. All I wanted was to take you out and do everything to make your life interesting. I didn't ask anything of you except to enjoy yourself, but you couldn't do that—you would make an issue of everything and now you're sorry for me. I don't want you to be sorry for me. I'm not sorry for myself."

" But I love you, Alonso. I always loved you."

This seemed to amuse him. " Oh no, you didn't and you don't. You aren't the sort who'd love anyone they considered a failure, whatever that may mean."

" But I never considered you a failure. Everything I said that day was nonsense. I'd had 'flu, I think, and it always leaves you a bit odd—I don't even remember what I said." This was a lie.

He shrugged his shoulders. " Well, what'll we do with ourselves until your train goes ? "

" We could have a drink. I've got fifty francs left besides money for the hotel."

" What an angel of goodness you are," he said, " how provident." But he accepted the offer.

Over drinks, Pernod for him and Dubonnet for her, she felt desperate and on the verge of tears. " Oh, why did you come to Saint Jean de Luz with me ? "

" I've told you. To gamble."

" To be beastly to me."

" To gamble."

" And what'll you do now ? "

" Go to San Sebastian, paint portraits, make some more money."

" And gamble it, I suppose ? "

There was no reply to this. She let her tears flow, not caring any more what the café proprietress might think. " Oh, please Alonso, don't go on gambling. Do go to Paris with Ignacio and then you can make something of your life."

" Poor soul," he patted her hand, " you certainly seem concerned about my welfare. Goodness knows what fearful picture of my decline and fall you've conjured up for yourself! "

He tried to comfort her and tease her out of her misery. He saw to everything, took the luggage to the station and put her on the train, firmly dissuading her from taking a later one. He sat beside her in the compartment, urging her to cheer up.

" But Alonso, do you still love me ? "

" You were quite right when you said I don't change. I don't."

" Well, then, it's all right, and we'll meet again in the summer."

He shook his head. " Whenever I've planned anything, it's always gone wrong, it's best never to plan. Let's leave it to chance and see what happens."

When it was time for him to be getting out, he pulled her up from her seat and put his arms around her, then he held her a little away from him and looked at her face. " No more tears, Marichu. Don't weep for me."

" And will I see you again in the summer ? "

" Let's leave it to chance." He kissed her tenderly and went out on to the platform. She opened the window and leaned out.

As the train moved off, he kissed her hand and smiled up at her. He bowed, waved his hand, then took out a handkerchief and waved with that. Through the smoke she could see him, large, solid, wrapped in his thick overcoat, waving and waving until he disappeared from sight.

PART FOUR

SUMMER 1936—AUTUMN 1937

1

TEN days before she was due to leave for Spain, Maria sent a postcard to Alonso announcing her arrival. There had been no communication between them since their last meeting and she therefore worded it very carefully, confining herself to the simple announcement that she would arrive in San Sebastian on a certain afternoon. If he wanted to meet her he could soon discover that there would only be one train coming through from Paris, if he didn't, he could assume he didn't know the time of the train. Also, once he knew she was there, he could phone the flat if he wanted to. The postcard itself suggested no intimacy, being a view of the Houses of Parliament—he would notice every little thing.

The day after this had been posted, Franco's military rising began. At first, it seemed almost certain that the Government would quickly regain control everywhere as one insurgent garrison after another was dealt with. It would all be over soon, thought Maria, because the main forces of the insurgents were in Morocco and would never be able to get through to the Spanish mainland. But soon fighting became more intense, alarming headlines of possible civil war glared from the daily papers, and she was forced to postpone her journey.

There had been no reply to her first postcard, and she could not possibly know whether he had met the train or not. She now sent a letter, asking him to let her know as soon as he could whether it would be unwise or not to leave for Spain. That, too, remained unanswered, although she had stressed the fact that he was the only person who could tell her what things were really like. Thinking that perhaps he might still be in Madrid, she sent another letter there, this time pointing out that to answer it could not commit him to seeing her. There was no reply.

Meanwhile, Miss Pearson had arrived in England and told her that she must be demented to dream of going to Spain at such a time.

Ever since 1934, Ethel had stayed on in the flat, acting as a companion to Miss Pearson, and also giving lessons to bring in a little pocket money. Although the pair of them never tired of criticising Spain and the Spaniards, they hated having to leave the country. Ethel had intended to stay on for at least another year or two, and Miss Pearson had meant to end her days there and be buried in a cemetery near her former patron. Now she felt she was being exiled, and vented her fury on the "Reds," as she called all Government supporters, holding them personally responsible for turning her out of her flat and forcing her to leave behind all her beloved pets and possessions made almost sacred through sentimental associations.

She now tried to make a home in the first two floors of a house belonging to a niece, and spent her time, angry and unhappy, nagging Ethel, fretting about Pomti Pom and the canaries, wondering if the "Reds" had killed them and imagining her flat overrun by a lot of hooligans who would destroy everything.

Shortly after their arrival, Maria was asked to tea. Sitting over a cup of "real English tea at last," their one consolation, in the shabby, colourless Bayswater drawing room, they talked of San Sebastian. There they had been able to look out on to the beautiful curved bay with the sea sometimes blue and calm, sometimes murky green and agitated, with the waves breaking against the tiny island of Santa Clara, from a spotless white stone balcony, in summer filled with bright flowers in pots. Here a dusty, black streaked balcony with its Victorian stone balustrade looked down on to dingy pavements and over on to tall, grey houses which blocked the light from the first two floors.

Already, Miss Pearson had appropriated the large tabby belonging to the house and kept it with her all the time. She spoke of getting a canary, but in spite of this, she knew she would never really like it in England, and she prayed constantly for an early victory for Franco and the restoration of the monarchy, when she would be able to return to a Spain more like what it used to be in the good old days. As she related the events which led up to their evacuation, she trembled with indignation and would have liked to embark on heated arguments with Maria as to whose fault it was. Maria was too conciliatory to oppose her for long. She felt sorry for the old lady, and shared her feeling of exile. Now that the situation was beginning to look so serious, argument seemed futile. Besides, she was genuinely glad to see them both, and on arrival had embraced them so heartily that they were taken aback.

Such opinions as Ethel held came from Miss Pearson, monarchist papers and the remarks of her pupils and their parents. She had little idea which side was which, and in particular could not place the Basque Nationalists because, although many of them were rich, respectable and fervent Catholics, they did not seem entirely behind Franco, and it was little wonder that she was mystified because at that time their position was far from clear. It seemed to her that on one side were the people, or rabble or mob, and on the other side were law and order or the police or the army or the aristocrats (anyone rich came under this last heading). When Maria pointed out, tactfully, " But surely the police, that is the Guardia Civil and the Guardia de Asalto, must have been on the Government side in most places and still are in all towns under Government control ? " The answer was, " Well, they seemed to be doing their best to keep order."

However, Ethel prided herself on her cool head and courage, and endeavoured to give as coherent an account as possible of their adventures.

For a long time back, ever since the Spring, there had been strikes almost every week, and much talk of trouble in the air. The sons and fathers of the families she taught went frequently over the border to Biarritz and St. Jean de Luz for secret meetings and conferences, and her pupils had often hinted that the " Reds " were not going to have things all their own way. Then came lurid reports of the murder in Madrid of Calvo Sotelo, the most prominent of the Fascist leaders, and the tremendous demonstrations staged by the Right at his funeral. All the monarchists and fascists of San Sebastian said quite openly that things would begin to happen now.

A few days later, on a feast day, after High Mass, Ethel and Miss Pearson heard two sharp shots and saw one of the congregation drop down on the porch of the church. Later, they heard he was killed. The following night, sounds of fighting woke Ethel at about eleven and continued all through the night. The next day they found, as they had so often found before during strikes, that they were confined to the flat. The wireless warned all who went on to the streets that they did so at their own risk. There were no papers, shops were shut. During the days that followed, things became more serious. Phone communication was cut off. Warnings were now issued over the wireless that people should not only keep off the streets, but also away from balconies and windows. The sound of fighting continued and they could hear machine-gunning from the other end of the Concha. They didn't know what they could have done for food if it hadn't been for Mercedes' enterprise and her association with the man in the grocer's shop downstairs. His shop was shut, of course, and he lived elsewhere, but every time he came along to feed the large collection of canaries he kept at the back of the shop, he slipped up to see if they wanted anything. " Between ourselves," said Ethel, " I think she was his mistress."

Then one morning they realised that the Antiguo, where they lived, was completely cut off from the rest of the town. Mercedes, slipping out early on one of her foraging expeditions, found the tunnel under the Royal Palace (through which ran the only road communicating with San Sebastian proper) sandbagged and guarded by military police, who would only allow through military and medical vehicles. " We in the Antiguo were in a very bad spot, because that was where all the aristocrats live — although many of them had fled over the border—and just the place the people would make for." Matters were not improved by having the local headquarters of the Gil Robles party in the basement.

All this time there was a heat wave. The shutters were closed in the drawing room. They could neither go out on to the balcony nor stand by an open window. It was stifling. Ethel felt she couldn't breathe. The wireless had to be kept on from morning till night, and between announcements there was a constant tic-toc, tic-toc which began to get on her nerves. Finally, she could bear it no longer. While Miss Pearson was having her afternoon siesta, Ethel crept up the ladder on to the roof to have a breath of air and change of scene. It was wonderful being out in the open air again. She was revelling in it, looking out to sea and over on to Igueldo, when she suddenly felt uneasy, and turning round saw a man at the top window of the house opposite pointing a gun at her. " I couldn't see his face, but I saw the gun all right. I was down that ladder in a flash, I can tell you. I thought my last moment had come! "

When Miss Pearson learnt what had happened, she was furious, and even now the thought of it still angered her.

" It was the most stupid thing to do," she said. " I'm amazed she wasn't shot. And, you know, if she had been, I should never, never have known what had happened to her, because I should never have dreamt of looking for her on the roof. Imagine what I should have gone through."

After that, she decided that they were now in great danger, and that she must really find the Union Jack and hang it out (she had been hunting for it for days). So the rest of the day was spent ransacking cupboards, turning out every drawer, looking in every corner. The whole place was turned upside down , but there was no trace of it. It was most extraordinary. They suspected Mercedes of stealing it, but her motive remained obscure. Miss Pearson was firmly convinced that only the flag could protect them.

The next day, three men came to search the flat. All pictures of grandees and royalty had been taken down and hidden, but they felt that this would only make things worse if a search resulted in their discovery, and they would both be shot on the spot.

" Really," said Ethel, " they were only boys of about sixteen, but very fierce and armed to the teeth. We wouldn't open the door. Mercedes talked to them through the grille and told them we were English. They said they *must* come in and search, they had orders. Miss Pearson said it was all my fault because I had been seen on the roof and they thought we were spies. They said they would break down the door if we didn't open it. So, finally, I went out and showed them a Union Jack I had hastily manufactured out of a red, white and blue striped jumper. It was an awful looking thing, but it did the trick. I explained that there were just the two of us, English ladies, and Mercedes. They seemed satisfied."

Maria laughed. " It wasn't the flag. It was your accent."

" They stood on the landing outside the flat playing with their guns, throwing them up in the air and catching them. I thought they'd go off by mistake. I kept opening the grille to see if they were still there, and every time they heard me, they'd say something and roar with laughter. Some insult, I suppose."

Things were desperate now because with the lads out there (they did not leave the landing till late at night, and came back first thing in the morning), Mercedes could neither go downstairs to look for the grocer nor could he come up to them, because they would have been suspected of conspiring with him to pass messages. There was very little food in the house, and, of course, no cigarettes.

The following day, a British warship, H.M.S. Verity, anchored outside the port, waiting to take away all the British who wished to leave. Ethel and Miss Pearson, hearing the front door bell ring, were terrified and nearly collapsed when Mercedes announced that a man had come to take them away. It was someone from the Vice-Consul's office in the Vice-Consul's car, and he had come to take them straight to the port. They had exactly two minutes in which to collect their belongings, because the Guardias were keeping the tunnel open for five minutes only. It was impossible to pack even one tiny suitcase in that time, and they were forced to leave with only their handbags, the clothes they had on and one or two dresses and coats slung over their arms.

" So you see what we've been through," said Miss Pearson. " I hope I never have such an experience again. All the ' Reds ' should be taken out and shot."

Maria tried not to laugh. " I can't see that they actually did anything awful to you."

" We were given some pretty black looks, I can tell you."

They were put down with the rest of the British colony at Biarritz, remained there for a time hoping against hope that all might blow over and they could return, and then, unable to afford the hotel expense any longer, made their way back to England.

" Times like these are terrible for people like us," said Miss Pearson.

" They're more terrible for the Spanish."

" Nonsense! They enjoy nothing better than fighting. It's one revolution after another. They brought all this on themselves when they let the King go. He'll be back on the throne before long, I can tell you. What they need is another strong man like Primo de Rivera ! "

Maria made no reply, stunned by the rush of visual and verbal memories which Primo's name evoked: a moonlight visit to a cemetery, a high, white wall, dark cypresses, the gleam of a carabinero's gun, a mouthful of silver teeth: Alonso's reply to the statement that in Primo's day everyone was so honest that you could leave a hundred peseta note out all night and it would still be there in the morning, " No, I should have taken it," she could hear this clearly as though Alonso was in the room beside her, and it made her laugh as she had laughed at the time: Pepe's thick hair as he buried his face in his hands, on her first morning in Madrid, telling them of the workers shot up in the Castellana by some of young Primo's gang: Antonio's gloomy face lighting in Baviera as he kissed the tips of his fingers and threw open his hand, a characteristic Spanish gesture, saying, " *Then* Spain was Paradise! " as he went on to describe the former elegance of the Court, the grandees in private trains, specially hired for them alone, speeding from South to North surrounded by every luxury, and feasting off lobster and champagne, on their way to join the King for the summer season. All these came not singly, but together like a montage picture.

She could hear Miss Pearson still holding forth, and waited until she had finished. " I suppose you don't know what happened to Alonso, that painter who did a drawing of Pomti Pom ? "

" I think I saw him downstairs in the house of one of my pupils," said Ethel. " I brushed past him as I came in, and he, stared at me and said ' good afternoon,' and I couldn't think who he was and then I remembered. I think it was him—a large, fat man, wasn't he ? "

" Did he say anything else to you ? "

" No, but he gave me such a stare."

" And that was this summer ? Then he's in San Sebastian."

" Yes. Of course, I can't be absolutely certain it was him . . ."

" What kind of a stare ? " She meant was it the stare of someone who knows he has seen a face before and can't place it, or the stare of a man who is suddenly confronted with a relation of the girl he loves. How could Ethel tell ? If she'd been there herself and seen it she couldn't have told. For one second she felt the delicious sensation again of being loved by Alonso, of being surrounded by his warm, benevolent, tender affection. The loss of this sensation was like pain. " But when exactly was this ? " she asked.

" About a week before all this started."

" And you brushed past him ? "

" Yes."

" Was he coming out of the door ? "

" I think he had just come down the stairs. He was in the passage, and I imagine he was just about to go out."

" And he said good afternoon ? "

" Yes."

" Nothing else ? "

" No."

" And did he stare at you for long ? "

" It did seem rather a long time."

2

Six weeks after San Sebastian had fallen, almost unresisting, to Franco's troops, and when Bilbao, as heroic in its defence as Irun had been, was the only Basque town of any size still holding out, news came.

One morning, on the mat below the letter box, lay a card, a glossy sepia card with touches of pink on cheeks and roses. It was a florally framed picture of a young couple. The girl was dressed in the style of the middle twenties, her dress was sleeveless, her waist line around her hips, her skirt above the knee, her hair a mass of close fitting tangled waves which looped like curtains over her forehead and hid the sides of her face. She glanced coyly sideways as she turned away from her sweetheart. The young man, in ill-fitting and shabby military uniform, looked at her meltingly. Below them was a rhyme:

"Though you must go while I stay here,
    Remember me dear."

(The metre was almost as bad as this in the Spanish.) Above the head of the girl was written in ink, " You," and above the young man, " Me."

On the back, in Alonso's pointed hand, was:

" Here I am in Burgos—a requete. Why don't you come out here as a nurse ? I can imagine you as one. Write to me."

He gave an address and the number of his regiment.

So there he was, on Franco's side, part of the Carlist militia, under the command of the sinister General Mola.

3

In September 1937, when the Basque provinces had fallen, when German and Italian intervention was becoming almost decisive in favour of the rebels, when the Government was still confident it would win because of its great victory at Brunete, Manolo arrived in London, Manolo who had first introduced Maria to Alonso.

He was there on his way to America as a special envoy for the Spanish Government. One of the first things he did was to arrange a meeting with Maria. It had to be short because it could only just be squeezed in between more important appointments. They met for tea in Harrod's restaurant.

It was a very different Manolo. She nearly failed to recognise him. His face was thinner and his hair greying. He rose and bowed as she came towards him.

" It's wonderful to see you again, Maria."

" Yes. I never thought we should meet again. Certainly not in London."

He smiled for a moment. " You weren't much of a correspondent."

He looked anxious, the ebullient manner was gone. She asked him how he thought things were going.

" Not too well at the moment. But I'm sure we'll win in the end."

" I've always thought the Government would win in the end, but it's turned into a fearful business."

He smiled again. " Let's talk of something else now."

" Tell me what *you* have been doing, first."

He had a splendid record and tried to make out that what he had done was nothing. His great regret was that he had not been in time to help in the defence of his own Basque province. As soon as news of the rising reached him in Shanghai, he set out for Spain. Arriving too late to take part in the defence of his own Basque country, since Irun had fallen and Bilbao was cut off from Government-held Spain, he made his way to Valencia. There he was refused permission to go to the front because the authorities thought his diplomatic qualifications might come in

useful somewhere else. For a long time he hung around feeling
he was doing nothing useful, until in the end he was allowed to
go and fight. He was wounded in the leg, sent back to Valencia.
" I got better and here I am."

" For long ? "

" A few days."

She longed to compliment him on the part he had played, but
knew it would only have embarrassed him. Like many other
Spaniards, he took physical courage as a matter of course and
the idea of an heroic death attracted him. Once, at a bullfight,
when she had expressed pity for the horse, he had answered,
" A glorious end to an inglorious life! "

" Now don't let's talk about the war any more. Tell me what
you have been doing."

" Well, I've been secretary of a Medical Aid Fund . . ."

" Oh, not that, Maria! Tell me other things. You've had lots
of young men, I suppose."

" Oh, *them*! "

He laughed at her disgusted expression. " I'm sure you have.
English girls are very flirtatious. I know that from Shanghai.
Very flirtatious and very cold. They never fall in love, do they,
Maria ? "

" I don't know. Some do and some don't, I suppose."

" And what about you ? Did you ever ? "

She shrugged her shoulders.

He persisted. " Don't think I'm flirting with you now, will
you ? But tell me, did you ever fall in love ? "

" I don't want to talk about love. I want to hear about Spain."

" And I want to forget about it—just for once. I shall have
it for the rest of the day, and to-morrow and the next day. I long
to talk about love. You might oblige me, Maria."

But she wouldn't. " There's nothing interesting to tell you.
What I really want to know is what became of all the people I
knew in Spain. Perhaps you could tell me." She paused while
she plucked up her courage and prepared herself for anything—
news that two-thirds of Alonso's regiment had been wiped out
on the Aragon front had reached her several months ago. " I'd
very much like to know what happened to your friend, Alonso.

Did you ever hear anything about him ? I heard somewhere that he was on Franco's side."

" Yes, he was. I'm not sure what's happened to him."

" You haven't any idea at all ? "

" I've had conflicting reports. First, I heard that he had been killed, and then I met someone who'd seen him sitting in a café in Burgos."

" And which do you think is true ? "

" My guess is as good as yours. The report that he was alive came last, so I daresay he is."

It was obvious that it had never occurred to him and never would that she had a more than friendly interest in Alonso. To Alonso every possibility would suggest itself, but to Manolo, Alonso may once have seemed a great man but never a romantic character.

" And did you ever hear of a Surrealist painter, a friend of his called Ignacio ? "

" I knew Ignacio very well. We were all at school together, though Alonso was a bit older. He died at Irun. All the defenders of Irun were heroes and they were nearly all wiped out."

She asked about all the others she could remember. Manolo seemed to know them all.

" Perez, the bullfighter, was caught in Seville. He's either still a prisoner there or else he's been shot by the Falange. Antonio is, of course, on Franco's side, he was probably in on the plot from the beginning, and so he was in Burgos when it broke out. He's doing propaganda."

" I can imagine it. He used to do it to me, about the Spanish tradition. And are Rafael and Jaime with him ? "

" No, they're both on our side, both fighting on the Aragon front. As for Pereda and Fuentes, I haven't come across any trace of them—they might have been killed in street fighting in the early days, or they may be doing guerilla warfare somewhere."

" Well, you can't expect to come across all your old friends."

" Usually one does come across them sooner or later if they're on our side, because Valencia isn't so big and the number of cafés is limited and they all turn up there when they're on leave."

" Poor Ignacio," said Maria, and shook her head.

Manolo didn't seem so sorry for him. Such a death was not a thing to pity.

" And can you imagine why on earth Alonso became a requete ? " she went on.

" I think I can. You see, you could be a Fascist or a Monarchist or a Carlist or a Basque nationalist or one of the many different kinds of Socialist, or you could simply be what we call a ' geographical.' I think a great many people were that. It simply meant that you were, or pretended to be, whatever your particular town was—you took the line of least resistance. Alonso was probably in San Sebastian when it fell and I suppose he went on as usual and then found himself in Franco's army." He shrugged his shoulders tolerantly. " It might have happened to anyone. Not everyone has strong political convictions, you know, and we can't all be heroes."

" Yes, I can see all that, but why on earth did he fight ? "

" He may have had no choice."

" And you were so sure he'd be on the right side when the time came."

" If he'd been in Madrid, perhaps he would have been."

She wondered would he have been in Madrid if it hadn't been for her ? He'd said he wasn't going to stay there when she left, and he'd come up all the way to St. Jean de Luz with her. No, he would in any case have gone to San Sebastian for the summer—he always did. " I'm sorry about it," she said. " He was very nice."

" Yes, he was a fascinating character, but very peculiar looking. I'm glad you got on with him. By the way, he was going to paint you and send me the portrait. What happened about that ? "

" He did paint it, but he didn't really finish it properly, because there was a general strike and I couldn't leave the house. He didn't think it would be worth sending it like that, so he gave it to me."

" And I was never told about this. Well, well."

" I didn't think it worth mentioning it in my letters."

" You wrote so few letters, and you hardly mentioned anything."

" There wasn't much to write about."

" And where's the picture now ? "

" In a cupboard."

" It would be interesting to have a look at it."

" If you have another spare minute before you go, I could bring it along." She thought for a moment. " I tell you what, Manolo, why don't you have it ? I don't want it and it might have historical value for you. It's very small and just a flat bit of cardboard, no trouble to pack. After all, it was meant for you."

" All right. I'd like to see it in any case. Was it good ? "

" Not very."

4

In a wine bar, over sherry, Maria handed Manolo the portrait, carefully wrapped in brown paper and tied with string. " It's quite small, you see."

" May I have a look at it now ? "

" I've packed it up. It would be rather a bother to undo it. You can have a look at it later."

He laughed. " You behave as though you're playing a joke on me. You seem very anxious I shouldn't see it before I take it away. I'll do it up again. Do let me have a look." He didn't wait for her reply. When it was unwrapped, the first thing he saw was the unfinished picture of some fishermen in the port which had been begun on the back. " He wasn't wasting any material, was he ? Just an old bit of cardboard he'd used before."

" He didn't really want to do it. He was bored stiff."

He turned it over and held it out at arms' length. " Very like you. Very, very like you. You haven't changed much. But

why did he put you in brown and green? You never had a
dress like that."

She laughed. "He made it up. He said 'rust colour and
green—typical English colours—Robin Hood.' I don't know
what he had in mind. Now you've seen it, do you want it?"

"You seem very anxious to give it away."

"I've never liked it much." She wanted to see the last of it.
It had been kept in a cupboard ever since she returned from
St. Jean de Luz. Every time she caught sight of it she could see
Alonso, fat and sleek, smiling, smoking a cheroot, drinking
pernod in one café after another in San Sebastian, composed,
smiling at her. It gave her a sinking feeling in the pit of her
stomach. "It was meant for you in the first place and you
ought to have it."

"All right. I'll take it with me. Do you want a last look?"

She leant against his shoulder as he held it away, and stared.
She saw the face of a sunburnt girl with shiny eyes and light
brown hair. As she watched, it kept changing as all pictures do,
sometimes seeming to smile and sometimes looking serious.
The girl was looking straight at her. Wherever you looked from,
her eyes were fixed on you. That was because she had been
staring at the painter, unable to take her eyes off him. If she
had not known it was herself, the portrait wouldn't have given
her the least idea of what the girl was like. Perhaps Alonso hadn't
had any idea of what she was like then. Later on, he always
made out he knew her better then she knew herself. He may not
have done, but she had taken his word for it. She looked away.

"This man who saw Alonso in a café, was he sure it was
him? Did he speak to him? How sure was he?"

"He wasn't in much of a position to speak to him. He'd been
taken prisoner and was being led through Burgos by his guards,
and on his way he saw some people sitting outside a café and
one of them was Alonso. This man escaped later and got back
to Valencia. That's how I know."

"And did he say how he looked?"

"No."

"Was he in military uniform?"

"He didn't say."

"There couldn't be anyone else who looked like him, could there?"

"I should be very surprised if he had a double."

"And what about the reports of his death? How definite were they?"

"One was from a cousin of his I met in Barcelona. He said he'd seen the announcement in a Burgos paper."

"But how had he seen a Burgos paper?"

"Biarritz and St. Jean de Luz are full of Spaniards of both sides and no side, you know."

"And what about the other report?"

"That was at second-hand from another man who said he had talked to a prisoner from the same regiment as Alonso."

"But both of these came before the man saw him in the café?"

"Yes, a little before. I didn't investigate the matter very closely."

She turned the picture over, wrapped it up, handed it to Manolo. They talked of other things, London, Shanghai and, once again, of old times in San Sebastian. Time flew by.

His eye caught the clock. "I must be off. I should have liked to have dinner with you on my last night, but it's business you know."

They parted at the top of an escalator. He kissed her hand. "Goodbye, Maria. We'll meet again in a better Spain."